Tracy's Landing

by
Shawn Zachary

Published by FICTIONWRITERS
in association with
LULU Publications

Cover Design
by
FICTIONWRITERS

Acknowledgments

A special thanks to all of my children
for the zany antics they pulled on
me during their upbringing.
It made this project a lot easier to write.

TRACY'S LANDING

CHAPTER I

The Transition

Cold rain pummeled the windows of a Greyhound bus as it sped north along the interstate highway -- pellets of water beating in harmonization with the drone of the engine and wheels churning against the pavement.

For what seemed to be endless hours, Tim Sawyer, a young gangly blond lad, thirteen years of age, sat mesmerized gazing out of his window at the blurred scenery.

"Are you all right, young man?" the elderly lady sitting in the aisle seat next to him asked.

It startled Tim to awareness. "Uhhh, . . . yes'um." He really hadn't been previously conscious of her presence.

She smiled as, for the first time, they made eye contact. "I've got some chocolate fudge my granddaughter made for me. Would you care to have some?" She took a round tin from her travel-bag in the process.

At first, shyness typical to one side of his personality surfaced. However, when the top of the canister was removed, seeing the large chunks of candy, literally chock-full of walnuts, it became too tempting to refuse.

"Here. Help yourself." She offered the container.

Tim chose one of the larger pieces. "Thanks."

"Now, if you would like some more, you just take as much as you'd like," she said, with a broad smile.

Tim sat quietly picking pieces off the fudge and savoring its rich taste. It was delicious. There had been very limited opportunities for luxuries in the recent past -- not since his mom and dad had died.

Dwelling on the sadness of his private world, he had never been away from Mississippi and felt desperately alone. He wanted to be as brave as his renown ancestor, and knew he wasn't afraid of a fight -- least, not with someone near enough his own size. But, suddenly becoming an orphan proved a bit more stressful than getting busted in the nose.

"Would you excuse me? I need'ta wash my hands." Tim stood, passing in front of his elderly friend to go to the restroom.

Walking down the aisle toward the back of the bus, he noticed there were very few vacant seats. Someone else occupied the facility when he arrived, so he simply waited his turn.

Once inside, he bathed his hands in lukewarm water and rinsed them with the cold. Cupping his hands to his mouth, he generously drank the thirst-quenching liquid.

As Tim turned to dry his hands and face, the bus suddenly lurched, throwing him against the outside wall of the small cubicle. He found himself being tossed around the room with every erratic movement of the out-of-control vehicle. In a matter of seconds -- which seemed like all of eternity -- the bus came to a harsh abrupt stop, crashing him against the forward panel.

For a brief moment, he sat dazed on the floor, trying to get his senses back together. The room tilted toward the right-side and front of the vehicle. There was little doubt they had left the road.

Finally standing, he leaned against the sink counter and tried to push the door open. The added weight, due to tilt, made it impossible. Bracing himself with his elbows, he placed both feet against the door and gave a tremendous shove. The door came ajar and wedged on the aisle floor, leaving an opening large enough for him to make a squeezed exit.

Mass confusion abounded. People were moaning and groaning while trying to untangle themselves from the debris and each other. The bus rested nose-first in a shallow ditch not too far off the road. Through the haze of mist and approaching dark, numerous other travelers were trying to assist from the outside.

"Aw, my Gawd," Tim said, as he remembered the friendly lady.

Attempting to get up the aisle was hopeless. He began to climb across the top of the seats until he reached his own. As he peered over, the lady had fallen to the floor between the seats. She bore a small cut on her forehead and her left arm was bleeding profusely.

With a bound, he leaped onto the seat, unzipping his jacket in the process. After pulling the tail of his shirt from his pants and yanking it over his head, he tore it into several pieces. Gently raising her, he wrapped the rags around her upper arm, making a tourniquet.

"Don't move, Mam. I think you got a broken arm and you shouldn't move, yet."

"Ooooooohhh," she moaned.

"The bus ran off'n the road. I can see flashin' lights. They'll be here real soon to help."

"Bless you."

* * *

All in all, it could have been much worse. The bus had come to its halt just feet-short of going over a steep embankment and into a stream. The majority of passengers escaped with minor cuts and abrasions. Tim suffered a slightly sprained wrist which sported a tightly wrapped ace bandage as a trophy.

Tim sat in the hospital emergency waiting room amid the other passengers. His timely nursing and application of the pressure wrap had saved the woman from an extensive loss of blood, and something possibly worse. He, like all those of his family before him, possessed an understanding of rivers and forests and the hazards they hold. Early training and experiences made him adept at coping with accidents and self-survival.

"You're quite a brave young lad," the bus driver said, as he stood in front of Tim, his arm brandishing a cast up to the elbow.

Tim looked up and blushed.

"The doctor asked me to let you know your lady friend will be okay. He also said your quick thinking may have saved her life. She has a compound fracture just above her wrist and they'll be keeping her in the hospital for a few days."

Tim responded with a weak smile, nodding his head in a positive manner.

"There'll be another bus here shortly that'll take everyone the rest of the way to Washington," the bus driver said, reaching down with his free hand to pat Tim on his shoulder.

As the driver turned to walk away, Tim found himself the center of attention as all eyes and flattering comments were directed at him. His face reddened even more.

By the time the group reached the D.C. depot, it was near ten o'clock in the evening, several hours past the scheduled time of arrival. Tim stepped from the bus and immediately became enveloped in the arms of a woman he didn't recognize -- it could only be Aunt Nell.

"Oh, good lord, honey, are you all right? Are you hurt? Oh, gracious me. Your hand?"

Tim didn't care much for all of the fuss. He felt exhausted and just wanted to get some rest. Shortly reaching the awaiting car, he crawled into the backseat and soon found sleep.

* * *

In the late hours of the dark night, a small cabin cruiser slowly became visible through the dense black mist of the Chesapeake Bay's inlet into Rockhold Creek. The craft made its way to Tracy's Landing Boat Yard where three men silently waited in front of a huge aluminum-sided structure. Two large doors slid apart as the boat entered a small channel and disappeared inside -- its waiting party joined the two arriving crewmen through another entrance.

Mr. Cash, sophisticated, but somewhat overweight, was dressed in a business suit reflecting a taste of wealth. He approached as the First Hand departed the boat. "Everything go all right?"

"Absolutely. . . . Went perfect. No problems at all," the First Hand said, handing Mr. Cash a small envelope.

* * *

From between slightly parted drapes, a slender beam of light shone across Tim's face. He abruptly sat upright in bed, gazing about the room. Everything seemed strange. He rubbed his eyes with the back of his hand, and for moments couldn't acclimate himself to the surroundings.

A loud quacking sound from outside could be heard -- unmistakably ducks. He was at Aunt Nell's.

Pulling the covers aside, he swung his feet to the floor and moved to the window. Shading his eyes from the brilliant sunlight, his pupils eventually adjusted from the dark.

"Oh, Gawd," Tim said aloud. "It's great out there."

Below the second-story view, sprawled a huge backyard

bordered by a long fence running across the rear of the property

-- on its other side, a gigantic marsh stretching to the edge of the Bay. To his right, sat another almost identical house to Aunt Nell's and a small marina with a boat sitting on a boat-rail next to a large shed. He noticed some activity on the piers, concluding it was a fisherman about to make way.

A knock on his door interrupted his survey. "Are you up?" he heard Aunt Nell call.

"Yes'um."

She poked her head into the room. "I've got some breakfast ready for you." Her head disappeared.

Tim hurriedly pulled on his clothes from the previous day, substituting a flannel shirt for the one he tore. Leaving his room, he found himself in a hallway with several doors at different intervals. One being the bathroom, he made a quick stop to do his morning business.

A stairway jutted downward from the hall's center. Having been so exhausted and sleepy when they had arrived the previous evening, he could remember very little of the home or even getting into bed.

The furnishings were old, like the house itself, but well kept. An upright player piano stood against one wall in the dining room, crammed behind a large oblong table surrounded by six chairs.

Aunt Nell anticipated his approach. "I'm back here."

"Oops," Tim said. "Forgot something. I'll be right there," he hollered, as he hurried back up the steps and reentered the bathroom. Wetting his hair with water, he used his fingernails to comb it flat against his head.

His second trip going down the stairs sounded like a herd of elephants.

Aunt Nell rushed from the kitchen to meet him. She frantically asked, "My gracious, child. Are you all right?"

"Yeah, . . . yes'um, I mean. What's wrong?"

Aunt Nell gave him a stern look. "With all that

thunderous noise, I thought you'd fallen down the steps. The house is no place to be a'runnin' like that. 'Specially on the stairs."

"Sorry, Aunt Nell. Didn't mean to scare you," he said, contritely, then altered his mood to include a great big grin. "That good smell comin' upstairs just made me want to get down here real fast."

Aunt Nell's frown quickly subsided. "Ain't you just the one?" she said, smiling. "You just mind what I say."

Tim followed his aunt into a large oblong kitchen, obviously built to the width of the house. Brightly colored flowered curtains adorned a string of windows across the rear wall, positioned above a counter spanning most of its length -- an electric range and sink interrupted its continuity.

Aunt Nell stood in front of the range, lifting eggs from a skillet to a plate. "Take any chair you'd like at the table," she said, without turning around. "And, after you eat, I want you to take a bath and get ready for church."

Fortunately, Aunt Nell apparently didn't notice Tim's sudden frown expressing his feelings on the matter.

There was a large pitcher of orange juice placed on the kitchen table with several plastic glasses stacked on top of each other. Tim took a chair nearest where he entered and sat down.

"I declare. You sure were a sleepy-head this mornin'." Aunt Nell carried a plate filled with sausage, eggs and toast to the table. "Help yourself to the juice. . . . Would you like some milk?"

"Yes'um. That would be good."

"You can get it from the fridge, if you got a mind to."

Tim arose, taking one of the nearby glasses and moved to the refrigerator. He found it jammed with vegetables, fresh fruit and other delectable items. He removed a carton and filled the tumbler just short of its brim and returned to his seat.

Everything smelled so good. He hadn't thought about

11

how hungry he actually was and delved into the plate almost savagely.

Aunt Nell sat across from him sipping a cup of coffee, facially expressing her delight with his pleasure over her culinary efforts. "If you'd like some more, I'll fix it."

"Aw, no Mam," he said, wiping his mouth on his sleeve. "This is fine . . . and really good, too."

"I've got some cold apple pie. How would that do?"

Tim quickly reacted. "Uummm. That could sure hit the spot."

Aunt Nell reached for a dome-covered plate sitting toward the far end of the table containing a deep-dish pie, two-inches thick with apples. She cut an oversized triangle wedge, and asked, "Is this big enough?"

"Oh, yes'um. It sure is." Tim finally broke the ice with a big grin and began to devour the dessert.

Slightly twisting in her chair, Aunt Nell seemed to be jockeying for position to pose a few questions.

Tim anticipated the coming barrage.

"I do declare, you've had a hard time of it. Haven't you, child?"

"No, Mam," he responded without looking at her.

"Oh, come now, dear. You don't have to be so brave. I know you've been under a strain since your mother and dad passed." Aunt Nell paused and changed her direction. "You'll like it here. There's a fine church; your school isn't very far away; there's a lot of odd jobs to make some spending money, and I'm sure you'll find a lot of good friends. The Elks Club has even got an organized league for junior sports." She took a long sip from her cup. "Do you like to play ball?"

"Yes'um."

"Have you ever played on a team?"

"Yes'um," he said, and added, "only for a short time. Just before my mom and dad died. I had to quit when one of my uncles took me in."

Aunt Nell sensed he had more to say and didn't want to risk having him retreat into his self-imposed denial.

"They lived 'cross town. I didn't have the chance to play on another team. Then, a few months later, I moved over to another kin's house, . . . and, then another, . . . then another." Tim stopped to gulp down the last piece of pie from his fork. "I miss my mom and dad. I don't want to move no more."

Getting up from her seat, Aunt Nell circled the table and knelt before Tim. "Oh, child. Oh, dear child." She embraced him with her arms. "You're home to stay."

Uncomfortable with his Aunt's attention, he pulled away. "I best be gettin' that bath."

CHAPTER II

Church Time

Tim dressed in his best slacks and a long-sleeve flannel shirt and met Aunt Nell in the kitchen.

"My don't you look snazzy," she smiled. "Are you lookin' forward to church?"

He lied, trying to sound enthusiastic. "Yes'um."

"You can go to Sunday School, too, if you'd like," she said.

"No, Mam. Church'll be just fine."

"Can't wait until you get outside and look around, can you?" She looked over her shoulder and grinned. "You're just like your Uncle James. Always gettin' into one thing or another. Couldn't sit still, he couldn't."

"Yes'um."

Tim milled around the house, plunking on the piano, reading the comics, and wishing he hadn't got dressed so early. When time came to leave, he was raring to go and get it over with.

Making a last minute pit-stop to take a pee, Aunt Nell was already at the car when he came busting out of the front door. He stopped at the top of the steps to comb his wet hair with his fingers.

"You hurry up, now," Aunt Nell called. "We're going to be late if you keep draggin' about."

Tim leaped from the porch to the ground, avoiding the steps. He rushed across the lawn, tripped and landed on all fours, dirtying the right knee of his pants.

15

Aunt Nell hurried around the car and met him as he arrived. "Lawd, a'mercy, child. You'll be the death of me, yet. Are you all right?" She started brushing him off and rubbed grass from his knee. "Just look at you. Just look at your pants. Lord, child. What am I to do?"

The church lot appeared to be packed when they arrived. Aunt Nell eventually parked across the street at a shopping mart.

The minister stood at the door welcoming parishioners as they entered. Tim was introduced and followed his aunt to a pew several rows from the front. He would have certainly preferred something more to the rear to be less conspicuous.

The reverend entered the pulpit and started service by selecting a hymn as everyone stood. Tim used the opportunity to subtly scan the congregation and made eye contact, making him feel as if he were looking into a mirror.

Directly across the aisle, sandwiched between two fat ladies, stood his almost double. For quite a while he pondered on deciding whether his look-alike was a boy or a girl. Dressed in jeans and a pullover sweater, with short bobbed-hair, he just couldn't tell for sure. Actually, he never did make up his mind until church was over.

After the end of benediction, the Pastor stood at the front door of the church meeting church members as they departed. Mr. Cash made his exit and stopped to talk to him as Tim and Aunt Nell approached.

"Nell. This must be your nephew I've been hearing about," the pastor said.

Aunt Nell acknowledged the minister with a huge smile. "Yes, he is."

"And, what is your name, son?"

"Tim, your . . . your Holiness."

They all broke into laughter. Aunt Nell became slightly flushed -- Tim extremely embarrassed.

"Reverend, will do," the pastor said, still smiling. "Well, Tim. I'd like to introduce you to Deale's Mayor Cash." The

16

pastor placed his hand on Mr. Cash's shoulder. "Mayor. This is your newest citizen and also our newest member of the congregation.

Mr. Cash reached forward and patted Tim on his head. "Welcome to Deale, Tim. I can always use another fine new voter." He began chuckling. "That is, when you've got a few whiskers on that chin."

Tim tried hard to suppress an immediate dislike of Mr. Cash, but made a subtle step backwards.

Aunt Nell took Tim by the shoulder. "Wonderful sermon, Reverend. Nice seeing you Mayor Cash.

Customarily, all of the old hens gathered out front to clack and gossip before going home. Aunt Nell took turns visiting one clutch after the other, eventually reaching a group where his aunt introduced him to Agnes Jamison.

"Henrietta, get over here for a minute," she called to her daughter.

"She's a girl," Tim muttered, disgustedly.

"What was that you said?" Aunt Nell asked.

"Aw, nothin'. . . . I was just talkin' to myself."

The young girl approached and stood by her mother with her shoulders slumped. "Henrietta, look up. . . . I said look up, Henrietta," her mother forcefully demanded. "This is Tim, Nell's nephew. She's going to be raising him from now on."

Henrietta nodded her head and turned, making a quick retreat.

"I'm sorry, Tim. She just doesn't have the kind of manners she should have," her mother said, apologetically.

Tim didn't respond.

"Well, Agnes," Aunt Nell said, "I best be getting home. Tim's all fired up about checking out the marina and I've got some shopping and a lot of baking to do for Wednesday's sale."

As they walked to the car, Tim sensed being stared at all of the way. However, when they drove past the church,

Henrietta was nowhere to be seen.

"That girl is something else," Aunt Nell commented, breaking the silence. "Just a head-strong child." She shook her head.

* * *

No sooner had the car came to a halt at the house, Tim jumped out and ran up the stairs to change clothes.

After investigating the yard and edges of the marsh, he spent a good while making a thorough inspection of the boat seen earlier. Finding an old rickety ladder leaning against the back of the marina shed allowed him to board the large vessel sitting on the boat rail. Tim estimated it to be some thirty-foot in length.

The upper-cabin, which housed the bridge, was open to the rear. A narrow entrance to a lower-area was centered below the windshield with the helm to the port. Below deck, he found a vee-bunk in the bow area, a dining booth that could be converted to sleep two, and a galley area with sink, refrigerator, and propane stove to the starboard side. Dust covered everything and a stench of mildew filled the air in the enclosure.

This is great, Tim thought. Why would anyone ever let such a fine craft go to pot?

Tim was rather knowledgeable about boats considering his age. His parents house had been adjacent to a rather large stream leading into the Mississippi, allowing him to spend numerous hours around the water and on their small wooden rowboat equipped with an outboard. He and his dad had built the boat just after he turned six years old. The experience and fun of the venture would always be a fond memory.

Having decided she was worth saving, at least for the purpose of making a good clubhouse, he proceeded to do a more thorough survey of the exterior and the hull. There were no gaping holes and the bottom seemed relatively sound.

18

Sated with his appraisal, Tim opted to take a stroll down the marina docks. As he walked along a pier, he came upon a slip where an elderly black man hovered over an engine set aft and below the boat's deck. Tim lifted himself to perch atop a piling and watched as the work continued.

Noticing Tim staring in his direction, the man nodded and returned to his work. After several moments, he got to his feet, wiping grease from his hands in the process. "Howdy," he said, interrupting the silence. "You must be Nell's new boy." He reached for a can of hand-cleaner. "Jasper's my name. What's yours?"

"Tim. . . . Tim Sawyer."

"Now, that's a fine name, if I ever heard one. When's did youse get in?"

"Last night."

"Jest takin' in the sights, I see." Jasper tossed his wipe-rag aside.

"Yep." Tim smiled with his response. "What'cha been a'doin'?"

"Aawww, this old crate needs some love'n' tender care from time-to-time. Jest puttin' in some spark plugs and tunin' her up. Know anything 'bout engines?"

"Yep, . . . and no."

"What'cha mean by that?"

"Well, I lived down on the Mississippi for a good while. We had a boat and I used to fish a lot with my dad. He taught me a bit about outboards. Don't know much about these big engines likin' you got."

"So, you's an old southern boy. Mississippi's a fine place. Got me some real ol' kinfolks lived down there." Jasper pulled a pipe from his pants pocket and pushed his finger down the chimney. Placing it in his mouth, he lit the packed tobacco. "Come on down here. I'll shows you a thing, or two 'bout these big engines."

Tim jumped from his perch and boarded the vessel.

"Now, first of all, dis is a fine ship," Jasper continued.

"Shes may not look as fancy as others, but it's what she's made of counts. Dis ol' lady is what theys call a bay-built boat. All's that means is she's been handcrafted, so to say, by some ol' salt down in dis area. They ain't made to be pretty. They's made to be good and do some hard work."

"Don't that cost a lot of money?" Tim asked, showing his sincere interest.

"Like's youse said a'fore. Yep, . . . and no. All 'pends on how's you gets the boat. Bay-built ain't made with all the fancy trimmin' on those rich-people's boats. She's a down-to-earth workhorse, but shes can still be a pride. Still, shes can be a good penny if'n she's new." He paused to drag a deep puff of smoke and started coughing and gagging trying to catch his breath. "Got's to give this up ones these days," he managed to say, finally getting fresh wind. "Theys say they ain't good for your health."

"So, why do you do it?"

Jasper gave a deep chuckle. "Now you sounds like my wife," he said, jokingly. "Looky here," Jasper said, changing the subject and pointing to the mast and paraphernalia. "This here's for doin' oysterin'. That's how I makes my livin' in the winter. I catches crabs durin' the summer.

Tim reached to test the strength of the tall pole protruding upward and marveled at its staunchness.

"Got's to be strong to stand the weight of that dredge and alls the oysters I pulls up." Jasper grinned. "Someday I'll lets you go with me, but it's some hard work. . . . Some real hard work.

"Who owns that big boat sittin' down there on the rail?"

"Your Aunt Nell. . . . Owns this whole marina, too."

Tim couldn't believe his ears. He couldn't have anticipated a better response.

"I sees youse got a lotta questions to ask. I'm finished my work, so youse just fires ahead."

"Who owns that rowboat with the motor for sale?"

"How comes she's got such a big house to live in? And, where'd she get all the money it's gotta take?"

"Boy, youse sure do have a bunch'a questions to ask." Jasper laughed, and hesitated to relight his pipe and take a deep puff. "Wells, you see. Your Aunt had a brother that owned all of dis. Whens he died, a few years back, it came to belong to Nell and your other aunt, Maggie. She lives in that other house right dere," he said, pointing to the structure sitting between Nell's home and the marina. "She's a bit older than Nell, . . . and crippled, too. Nell does some to take care a her, but she's got a nurse that comes in a good deal to help. As far as the boat for sale, I owns that. Why? Youse wanna buy it?" He laughed again.

"Wow. I never knew none of that."

"Well. Seems you ain't had too much time to find out." Jasper grinned, baring his bright-white teeth. "They ain't got a whole lot'a money, but they's not hurtin' much, neither. "'Tween the income theys gets from rentin' out to us boaters and the two other houses theys owns up the road, they's doin' okay." Jasper took the pipe from his mouth and banged it in the middle of his palm.

Tim took particular notice that Jasper walked to an ashtray on the dash to empty his hand of the tobacco.

"Let's me tell you somethin' 'portent. Dis here bay's got too much junk in it that it don't need. Peoples been pollutin' dis water for way too long. Theys taken most of the big fishes from the water, . . . not bys fishin', but bys killin' 'em off like crazy peoples, dumpin' anythin' and everthin' they do."

Tim sensed the concern and anger in his mood.

"Don't likes to sound so mean." He softened his voice. "But, I can't tells youse how much youse gotta be careful about what's put in the water. Don't ever put nothin' in her that don't belong dere."

"Yes, sir."

Jasper smiled broadly. "You's a good lad. I gots no

doubt yous'll take good care."

Tim heard a loud buzzer in the distance. "What's that?"

"That be your Aunt Maggie. She rings it when she's wants some help."

"Aunt Nell's gone shoppin'. Should I get up there?"

"Ain't gonna hurt a thing if'n you do. . . . Not a thing."

Tim scurried off the boat, running toward the persistent blasts of the buzzer's sound. After reaching the front door of the house, he knocked out of usual protocol.

"Dummy, I can't come to the door. Get in here. I need help."

Somewhat befuddled, Tim entered and observed a very old lady stranded halfway up the staircase sitting in an elevator chair.

"Who might you be?" she asked. "Oh, never mind. Just get me off this contraption. It stopped on my way down and I couldn't get it started again."

Without hesitating, Tim rushed to her. On second thought, he paused. "Mam. I don't think I'm strong enough to get you up or down these stairs."

"So, what good are you for, anyway?" she harshly responded, and then began to pout.

At that moment, the screen door burst open and a young man entered the vestibule. "Maggie. What in the world are you trying to do?" he asked, coming up the steps two-at-a-time.

"Harper. Is that you, Harper? It's about time someone showed up," she said in a disgusted manner.

"Now, calm down, Maggie. We'll have you out of this in just a few minutes."

Tim felt totally confused.

"Hi. I'm one of Nell's roomers," he said, introducing himself to Tim. "I don't think you remember, but I drove you home last night from the bus. Don't be shook up. This kind'a thing happens every once in a while."

"I'm sorry," Tim said. "I couldn't help her by myself.

She's so old ."

"Old? I ain't old," Aunt Maggie contradicted, her voice fading with the response.

"Don't pay too much attention to what she says. She has periods of delirium. Sometimes, they don't last very long." Harper carried her back up the stairs and to her bedroom, placing her beneath the covers. "Now. You stay here like a good girl." He smiled, kissed her on the forehead, and turned to confront Tim. "She's really a great old gal. Just a bit unpredictable at times." He crossed the room and closed the drapes. "Why don't you stay with her until her nurse gets here?"

Tim nodded his agreement as Harper took his leave, waving a hand goodbye.

Aunt Maggie rested passively as if asleep. "So, you're my nephew, Tim."

Startled, Tim stuttered his reaction. "Ye . . . Yes'um."

"Don't be so shy. Come over here and let me get a good look at you."

Tim moved closer, standing against the side of her bed. His aunt reached and took his hand in hers.

"You're a fine young man. You look somewhat like your mother. Oh, I remember her." She tightened her grip in little squeezes. "Don't you let that fuddy-duddy old sister of mine be too strict on you."

"Thank you for being here, but you'd better go."

A voice from behind startled Tim. He spun to face a rather tall large-boned woman dressed in a white and red pin-striped uniform.

"She's had a bit of stress and should get some rest." The nurse smiled and stepped aside from the doorway.

Tim turned to say goodbye, but Aunt Maggie had fallen asleep. He tenderly released her hand and placed it gently on the bed.

"Come see her tomorrow. I'm sure she'd love that."

CHAPTER III

The Rail Boat

As Tim left Aunt Maggie's house, he noticed Aunt Nell driving up the road and met her as she pulled into the driveway. The rear seat was loaded with packages and plastic bags.

"Hi, dear. Have you had a good day?" she asked, while getting out of the car.

"Yes'um. I sure have." He filled his arms and carried several bags into the kitchen. Aunt Nell immediately began to unpack the groceries while Tim made several more trips. "Is there anything I can do to help?" he sincerely asked, as he squeezed into a chair sitting close to the table.

"No. You sit right there for a minute until I get this meat put away. I bought some things for you." She began packing the freezer in the pantry. "On second though, you can fold up those grocery bags for me and put them under the sink."

"Nell," Harper called out, as he entered the room. "Did you get those VCR cables I needed?"

"Sure did," she responded, closing the pantry door. "They're laying over there on the counter."

"Great," he said.

"Harper. You didn't get a proper introduction last night. I'd like you to meet my nephew, Tim."

"We've already met, proper. Over at Maggie's a little while ago." Harper nodded his head in the direction of the house next door.

"Oh, Lawdy. Was she at it, again?"

"Yep. As usual. Got stuck halfway down the stairs in her seat. Tim heard the buzzer before I could get there."

"Harper is one of my roomers. Jeff is the other, but he's working today," she explained to Tim.

"See you later, Tim," Harper said, as he grabbed the cords and walked past. "I rented a couple of good movies. Maybe you'd like to watch them with me later."

"Yep. I'd like that, if you don't mind." Tim smiled in approval.

"No problem. Catch you later."

"You seem to getting along fine." Aunt Nell smiled and began sorting through the other packages until locating her intended items. "Here. How do you like these?"

Tim's eyes popped wide-open as she handed him a couple of pairs of Levi's. "Wow. I've always wanted some of these."

"Go try them on. I'm pretty sure they'll fit," Aunt Nell said, expressing pleasure at his delight.

As she returned to tend other duties at the sink, Tim's enthusiasm with his new duds was so intense he ignored propriety and dropped his pants on the spot.

"Lawd, a mercy, Tim. I'd think that you might have a bit more . . ." Originally shocked by Tim's disregard for personal privacy, Aunt Nell caught herself, realizing his boyish innocence. "More . . . more meat on them bones to fill them out just right," she said, as she moved to check the space around the waist band. Reaching for a shoe box, she handed it to Tim.

"Oh, my Gawd, . . . they're Nikes."

"Now, you watch your mouth, young man, I know you're excited, but you be careful how you go using the good Lord's name." Aunt Nell's frown changed to a smile.

26

"You really do like them, don't you?"

"Oh, yes'um. Mores than I could ever tell. Everythin' else, too. But, it all costs too much money."

"You liking them is what counts. That's what money is for," Aunt Nell said, beaming with satisfaction.

Tim unexpectedly gave his benefactor a huge hug.

"Now, that's worth a million dollars," she said, kissing him on the forehead. "You go wash up for dinner and then come on back here and keep me company while I get it ready."

Tim wiped his forehead with his sleeve and started to leave.

"Not so fast," she said, halting his departure. "Take all those belongings with you to your room. I'll put them away later."

Backtracking, Tim laded his arms with a huge pile -- making a few trips to complete the chore.

Dinner proved delicious, consisting of homemade beef stew, coleslaw, and lots of hot rolls with peach pie as dessert. Harper and Jeff were both present at the meal and departed shortly after eating.

Aunt Nell poured herself another cup of coffee and returned to the table to finish her pie. "Would you like some more?" she asked Tim.

"No, Mam. It sure was good, though."

"So long as you keep liking my cooking, you'll make a lot of points with me," she said, laughing. "Well, why don't you tell me about all the things you did today?"

"I met Jasper. He's a real nice man. He said I could go oysterin' with him one day and he showed me a lot of things about his boat."

"That's fine. Jasper is a good God-fearing man. You'll do well by being friends with him. He knows more about the water and boating than just about anybody." She sipped her coffee.

Tim opened a box of toothpicks and began toying with

them. "Aunt Nell. Jasper said you owned that big boat down on the rail. Is that true?"

"That old thing? It belonged to your Uncle James' before he passed. He had it sitting there working on it when he disappeared. Just didn't do much about it after that."

"Why did he disappear?"

Aunt Nell suddenly reflected some melancholia which slowly changed to a smile. He's been gone now about three . . . no four years. Some say the devil got his due.

Tim knocked over the log cabin he was building. "I don't understand."

"I'm sorry, dear. It's just that your Uncle James didn't make a lot of friends. Oh, they respected him for his work, all right. But, people just didn't understand him very well. Can't say I blame them, altogether."

Aunt Nell rose, carrying her cup and plate to get a refill. "He'd been just working on that powerboat out back so's he could sell it. His real love was big sailboats and clipper ships. I remember him as a boy and talking crazy dreams about going around the world some day."

"How did he die?"

"He drown. . . . Least that's what everyone says. He'd got to the point he'd go off for days at a time. Then, a terrible storm came up. Some think he went out to the ocean. They never found a trace of him. . . . He never came back." Aunt Nell wiped the corner of her eyes with her apron. "Well, enough of that. It's long over with.

Tim started putting the toothpicks back in the box. "Jasper said you and Aunt Maggie own all this property, and the marina, too."

"He's right. James left all of it behind. Your uncle never married and he was a real craftsman with boats. That's what those two big sheds are for down at the dock. And, he and our Dad built these two houses." Aunt Nell paused to sip more coffee.

"Would it be okay if'n I do some cleanin' up on the boat.

It'd be fun spendin' some nights out there. You know, like a clubhouse. . . . Maybe, someday, I could even get her ready for the water."

"Now, what would you be knowing about fixing boats?"

"Fore mom and dad passed, we lived right on the water. Dad taught me an awful lot 'bout boatin'."

"Uummmm, I don't know . . ."

"Please. I promise I'd be careful."

Aunt Nell broke into a huge smile. "Well, since you like my cooking so much, tell you what. Why don't I just give you that old boat?"

Tim couldn't believe his ears. "You mean it? You really mean it?" he repeated, excitedly.

"Sure do. So long as you're careful and don't go getting yourself in trouble."

"Oh, man." He gave himself a high-five above his head.

"I don't know how many tools are left down in the shed. Some of them have been sold or taken," Aunt Nell said. "Whatever you find is yours."

"Oh, wow. That's great." Tim became so hyper there was no way he could sit still to watch a movie, no matter what it happened to be. He stopped long enough to thank Harper for the offer and wasted little time getting outside to use the hour of remaining daylight.

"Now, you just be remembering you've got school tomorrow," Aunt Nell said, as he hurried out the back door.

After making another brief survey, Tim got several items from the house, plus another caution about the cold night air and not to stay out too late. He returned to the boat loaded with cleaning equipment and supplies. Concentrating mostly on the dining booth area and wiping away dirt and dust, he decided a more thorough job could be done later.

By the time he finished, it was getting pretty dark. Basically satisfied for the time being, he sat in the booth and lit a candle he had brought from the house. Armed with a pencil and notepad, Tim began making a list, itemizing each and every thing needed to be done.

Fortunately, none of the glass was broken, and the interior not too bad for the most part. However, by the stains left in the wood, he detected a few places that had been leaking.

Tim sat back in the corner and stretched his legs across the bench seat. He closed his eyes and visualized how beautiful his boat could be. His mind filled full with fantasies and dreams.

"Hey, big buddy," Harper said, as he shook Tim's foot. "It's cold in here. Nell's a bit worried that you're okay."

Tim had fallen asleep. "What time is it?" he asked, as he stretched his arms.

"Almost eight o'clock."

"Okay. . . . Thanks." Tim slid to the end of his seat.

"No problem. But you better get a move on before your aunt goes on the warpath."

* * *

Unlike weekends and holidays, getting up on a school morning was a real bummer. Sleepy-eyed and yawning, showering and getting dressed constituted a terrible chore. Making this first day even worse was having to be driven by Aunt Nell so she could enroll him. From experience, he didn't relish having to go through the ogling and embarrassment.

Tim fiddled with the food on his plate, his appetite suddenly deserting him.

"You should eat your breakfast, Tim," Aunt Nell said. "I don't want you getting sick on me."

"I'm not too hungry this mornin, Aunt Nell."

"I know it's a big day, and you probably got the jitters, but you should really get something on your stomach."

Tim nibbled some more and at least finished a glass of milk.

CHAPTER IV

Confrontations

Showing little gusto, Tim climbed into the car's front passenger seat as Aunt Nell got behind the wheel. As they neared their destination, an unusually tall monstrous bald man, sporting scars on his face and head, crossed the road in front of them forcing Aunt Nell's car to come to a halt. He glared menacingly at them through the windshield. Aunt Nell calmly waved him to cross, but the giant's evil stare made Tim wince and cower in his seat.

"Aw, my Gaw . . . gosh. Who is that?" Tim was still shaken.

"That's just Skull."

Skull moved slowly away as Aunt Nell turned into the school's parking area. They got out of the car as the bell rang. The majority of kids were already inside, headed for their home rooms.

After going straight to the office, Aunt Nell approached the school clerk and began filling forms and signing documents.

"Well, that should do it," the school clerk said. "Tim's all set for his first class." She walked around the counter and handed Tim some papers. "Here's your schedule.

You'll find your first assignment just down the hall and to the right. Give these other forms to your teacher." She provided an almost mechanical smile. "Welcome to Deale Middle-School."

Aunt Nell followed Tim out of the office and into the hallway where several kids were late for class. Aunt Nell leaned down and kissed Tim on the cheek before he realized what was happening.

Absolutely embarrassed, he wiped his cheek with the back of his hand as the kids walked by giggling and snickering. Tim waved a weak goodbye and walked down the hall.

After locating his destination, Tim paused outside of the door gazing through its glass panes. Inside, a mixture of about twenty boys and girls were seated at student desks, and the teacher stood at the front of the class wiping the blackboard.

He opened the door and entered, all eyes present focused on his arrival.

"You may take any available seat you choose," the teacher said.

Tim simply nodded an affirmative response and selected one near the rear. A stir in the classroom followed, with mumbled conversation and comments between students.

Before sitting down, Tim turned and blurted out, "I got this stuff . . ." Tim dropped his lunch bag, as the papers intended for the teacher slipped from his hand to the floor.

The class started laughing.

Tim's face reddened.

"Okay, class. That will be enough. Come to order," the teacher demanded, as Tim quickly gathered his items and placed his lunch bag on his chair. "Bring the papers to me, please."

Tim reluctantly moved to the front of the classroom and handed the forms to her.

"Thank you," she said, and continued as Tim turned to

walk away. "Just a moment before you return to your seat."

Tim halted in his tracks and sheepishly walked back toward the front of the room as the teacher glanced at the office papers. "Well, Tim. Why don't you introduce yourself to your new classmates and tell them where you're from?"

"Aw, do I really have to?"

"Yes, you most certainly do."

Tim reflected an uneasy distress, fumbling for words, while facing the class. With his head slightly lowered, he barely audibly mumbled, "Tim Sawyer . . . Mississippi."

"You can do better than that."

This time he blurted it out loud and clear. "I'm Tim Sawyer and I come from Mississippi." He immediately scurried back to his place and flopped into his seat, smack-dab on top of his lunch.

Squirming for a moment, he embarrassingly pulled the sack from beneath his rump and shoved it into his desk. His classmates roared with laughter.

After a long morning, lunch-break came and Tim truly welcomed the respite.

The cafeteria was nearly chaotic with students in the food-line, while others scrambled for seats. Seeking isolation, he located a spot where he could be alone. He opened his rumpled lunch bag and pulled out two smashed sandwiches and a mashed container of potato chips.

Preoccupied with eating, he didn't notice the approach of three boys his age.

"Hey dude. Mind if we join ya?" one of them said. "My name's Smudge. This here's Smoke . . . and that's Frog."

"What the heck kind'a names them supposed to be?"

Frog responded in a scruffy voice, "Nicknames. Ain't you got one?"

"Nope," Tim said, showing disinterest.

"Smoke got his name cause he runs fast," Smudge said. Frog got his from . . ."

Tim interrupted him. "Yeah, I know. Cause of the way he sounds."

"Yeah, and those inch-thick glasses on his fat nose," Smoke added.

Frog leaned over his tray, his mouth crammed with food, spitting it as he spoke. "Up yours, skinny ass." Tim made a fake vomiting gesture at Frog's performance. All four youths giggled and returned to munching their food.

Smudge looked up at Tim. "Hey, dude. You're okay."

Tim cracked a sly grin.

The midday break having come and gone, and most of the afternoon session, as well, Tim eyed the huge clock on the classrooms side wall as the minute hand reached two-forty-four. A slight buzz began to emanate among some of the students. As the hand clicked to two-forty-five, a bell loudly rang. Tim sprang from his seat.

"Tim," the teacher called loudly over the commotion. "You can sit down."

Totally confused, Tim slowly slid back into his seat. The remaining students snickered and giggled.

"The first bell is for students riding the school buses," the teacher said, in clarification.

Tim slumped in his chair.

Fifteen minutes later the second bell rang and Tim was soon exiting the front of his new school. "Dang it," he said, with a sigh of relief.

Smudge called out to Tim. "Hey, dude. Wait up,"

Tim stopped to wait for his three new associates to catch up.

"Which way ya goin? Where ya live?"

"East-Side Marina. . . . My aunt owns it."

"Aw, man. You got it made," Frog said. "Wish my folks owned somethin' like that."

"Come on." Smudge urged Tim. "I'll show ya a shortcut."

The four youths headed in a direction around the side of

the school toward a large sports field behind the building. As they passed a group of kids, Tim noticed Henrietta nearby. He waved to her, and called out, "Hey, Henrietta. How ya doin'?" Tim turned his back, walking a few steps further.

"Auuh, oooh," Frog said. "Shouldn't ought'a done that."

Tim felt the impact of someone pouncing on him from behind, sending him to the ground. He twisted underneath the weight and received a fist against his cheekbone after managing to get to his back. A wrestling match ensued, with Tim eventually sitting atop Henrietta. "What the . . . . What the hell's wrong with you? You crazy or somethin'?"

"Don't you call me Henrietta," she said, gritting her teeth.

"It's your name, ain't it?"

"No," she said, emphatically. "My name's Hank. And, don't you forget it. Don't you ever call me Henrietta." Getting to their feet, Hank spun on her heels and stormed away brushing herself off.

Tim's three cohorts quickly gathered around. "Man, she's one tough broad," Smoke said, shaking his head.

"You should'a hit her," Frog said, adding his opinion.

"Yeah. If it had been me, I would'a busted her chops," Smudge said, showing a fist.

"Bullshit, Smudge. Ya know she can lick the crap outta ya."

Smudge blushed and shoved Smoke in the chest.

They all started laughing as Frog threw some sparing punches.

* * *

Mr. Cash exited the front of an office building across from the State Capitol and immediately got into a stretch limousine. Inside the limo, he sat with his back to the Chauffeur. A middle-aged man, Garcia, and a second younger one, both of Latin American decent, sat across from him -- all three dressed in stylish business suits. The

35

younger man, Roberto, opened a custom built bar and filled two glasses with ice and a generous portion of Chivas Regal Scotch. He handed one to Mr. Cash and the other to his older counterpart.

The senior Latino offered a toast. "To your success."

"Our success," Mr. Cash said, in correction.

The limousine pulled from the curb and blended in with traffic exiting to the south of the city.

Eventually entering an industrial area fronted by the South River, they reached a large factory/warehouse built directly on the water's edge. A huge loading platform to the left held boxes being unloaded from two eighteen-wheelers.

After coming to a halt in front of two sliding doors, the chauffeur beeped the horn and waited for them to be opened. The vehicle pulled inside and the three rear occupants exited the limo, then proceeded toward the back of the structure between high stacked rows of cartons and boxes.

As they approached the back wall, sounds of machinery coming from beyond a partitioned area became increasingly louder. At the rear, they entered a factory environment workshop with about fifteen employees dressed in white uniforms performing various tasks. A sleek fiber-glass shell of a twenty-five foot boat sat in a cradle as workers tended to it.

The head engineer, Crowley, approached Mr. Cash and shook his hand as the latter introduced him to the visitors -- their voices inaudible due to the loud noise. Crowley motioned for them to follow him to an enclosed office area.

Once inside, with the door closed, conversation became much easier. They crossed the room to a large drafting table where blueprints were spread about.

Mr. Cash stood next to Crowley as he explained the drawings. Cash turned to his elderly guest and asked, "Now, what do you think of my investment?"

"Outstanding. Ingenious," Garcia said, expressing a huge smile. "When will it be ready?"

Mr. Cash looked at Crowley for a response.

"Four . . . maybe five weeks at the most," Crowley said.

Garcia gave a look of pleased approval and a gesturing nod of his head.

Mr. Cash accepted his reaction with great enthusiasm and asked, "The deal's done?"

"Done," Garcia agreed.

The two shook hands and exited the office as the others followed. The loud noise again filled the area and Crowley waved his hand in a goodbye gesture as he watched them leave. Crowley walked to the boat shell and rubbed his hand in a gentle manner and patted it, exuding a broad smile.

* * *

Tim, Smudge, and Frog climbed down the ladder from the rail-boat. As they reached the ground, Smudge said, "Man. It's a shame Smoke had'ta get home and didn't see this. You're sure one lucky dog, Tim."

Tim responded, with a big grin. "Thanks."

"I gotta get home," Frog said. "My ol' lady's gonna be pitchin' a fit."

"Mine, too," Smudge said, in agreement. The two lads took off in a run.

Tim felt pleased with himself and his new found friends. As he returned to retrieve the keys to the marina shed from the house, he ran into Aunt Nell.

"Where are you off to so fast? As if I didn't know."

"I'll be at the boat."

"Just a minute, now. Do you have homework to do?"

"No, Mam. She didn't give us none."

Tim flew out of the back door in a flash.

He propped the double-doors of the larger shed wide-open affording sufficient light for his search. Inside, he found numerous paint cans aligned on shelves and a broad selection of various types and sizes of lumber. Closer investigation proved most of the paint had hardened. He did locate some usable stains and polyurethane.

In the smaller structure, he ran into more luck. There were several different hand-tools, including screwdrivers, a hammer, a rusty handsaw, and numerous screws, nails and other miscellaneous repair items. He also found a wheelbarrow which he used to transport a great deal of things to the boat.

He heard Jasper call out to him.

"You sure is a'workin' kind'a boy. Come on here for a minute."

Tim closed the shed doors and went down to the dock.

"Them's tools you found isn't all that good. I got some electrical ones you can use at my house."

"That's super," Tim said, showing great exuberance. "Aunt Nell gave me the boat."

"Did she? Now, I think that's 'bout a fine thing to do. Been a long time since Captain James left that fine lady sittin' alls alone on that rail. 'Bout time she's goin' get some love-n-tender care."

Containing his enthusiasm was impossible. "Oh, wow. I can't hardly believe this is all true. Do you think she could sail again?"

"Whoa, now. Back up a bit. Does you got any idea how much work it'd take to get her seaworthy?" Jasper clearly noticed the sudden downturn in Tim's spirits. "But, ain't impossible."

Jasper changed course, as did Tim's frown. "Her bottoms in good shape, last time I seen. . . . May need some caulkin' here and dere. She's gonna have to sit in the water for a good spell 'fore she swells back up."

"Do you think I can do it?" Tim implored.

"Youse jest keep a'workin' hard as youse been doin' and it wouldn't go suprisin' me none."

"Thanks, Jasper. . . . Thanks a whole lot."

"You come down here tomorrow after schools and gets the tools I told you 'bout."

"You bet'cha. I'll see ya then." Tim scurried up the pier

and toward the house as happy as a lark.

Josh and Harper sat at the table as Tim entered the back door. Aunt Nell finished putting dinner on the table and for the first time noticed Tim's eye.

"Lawd, a'mercy, child. What happened to your face?

"Aw, uhhh . . . me and some guys was jest goofin'-off and I got bumped a good one."

Harper exuded a sly smile, a slight nod, and a wink of his eye at Tim as Aunt Nell took her seat and began passing and dishing food.

"I noticed you had some friends out back."

"Yes'um. I met 'em at school."

"Well. After you finish dinner, you best be putting a cold rag on that eye."

Tim hadn't been totally truthful earlier to Aunt Nell. He did have homework to do and by the time he finished it after dinner, his clock showed the hour to be much too late to go back to the boat.

CHAPTER V

Friendship

The following morning, Tim's room was in disarray -- clothes thrown across the back of the chair, tennis shoes and socks strewn on the floor, and wadded paper scattered from having missed the waste basket.

In evidence of the early a.m. hour, sunlight seemed determined to get past the window blinds as the alarm clock rang its unwelcome sound. The hands read six-twenty-eight.

Tim rolled over and reached to shutoff the noisy disturbance sitting on the night stand next to his bed. He scooted to the edge of the bed, touched his bad eye, and groaned.

In the bathroom, Tim stood at the sink gazing into the medicine cabinet mirror. His eye proved to be swollen, black and blue. "Oh, wow. What am I gonna do?" He tenderly splashed cold water against his face.

Not having any luck with his attempt to get the day off, Tim walked to school using the shortcut he had been shown. He heard someone shouting from a distance.

"Hey, Tim. Wait up."

Tim stopped and turned to see Smoke running after him.

He reached Tim out of breath and wheezing. "Whew, man. You sure got a doozy."

"Yeah. Jest my luck."

They continued walking together toward school.

"Sorry I couldn't make it by your place yesterday. My

ma's gotta be at work by four. I had'ta baby-sit.

"Ya gotta do that every day?"

"Yeah, 'til my dad gets home."

Smudge and Frog were milling around on the front school steps as Smoke and Tim approached.

"What's goin' on?" Smoke asked.

Smudge noticed Tim's eye. "You're a cool dude."

"Yeah. A real cool dude," Frog said in agreement.

Smudge slapped Tim on the back and placed his arm around his shoulders as they walked into the building. "You sure put ol' Hank down. Nobody around here done that before."

"Aw, forget it, will ya? She's jest a dumb girl."

"We better get to class before the bell rings," Frog said.

Kids packed the hallway. The school counselor, a short chubby, in her late thirties lady, with horn-rimmed glasses stood just outside the school office. "Tim Sawyer. . . . Just a moment, young man. The Principal would like to see you."

"Aw, sheeeet," Frog said.

Tim offered a thumbs-up sign. "See ya guys later." He followed the counselor through the office door. She motioned for him to take a seat.

Hank already sat in one of the chairs along the wall. He chose a seat of his own, several places away -- neither acknowledging the other.

About twenty minutes passed before the school clerk appeared. "The Principal will see the two of you, now."

Tim and Hank got up at the same time and headed for the principal's office door. Hank arrived first and opened it and, stepping aside, said, "After yooouuuu, sir."

Tim brushed past and into the office, Hank following close behind. As distasteful as it was, they were forced to stand beside each other confronting the principal, as he sat on the other side of his desk.

"I'm sure you both know why you're in my office this

bright and sunny morning." He seemed to pause in expectation of a response, but got none. "I expect to hear all about yesterday's entertainment in the school yard."

They both stood silent and unresponsive.

"Well, don't both of you rush to talk at once. Why don't I hear from you first, Ms. Jamison?

"I . . . I . . ."

Tim interrupted Hank's response. "Sir. It be all my fault. I was showin' off and said somethin' I think must'a offended her."

"And, what might you have said?"

"I don't know, Sir. I really cain't remember too much about the conversation."

"And you, young lady. What have you to add?

"Nothin', . . . Sir."

Tim tried to subdue his shiner by lowering his head.

"I suppose that's how you got your black-eye, Mr. Sawyer?"

"Yes, Sir. I think I bumped it on a rock on the ground when we was wrestlin'."

"Hummmmph!" The principal paused for several moments tapping a pencil against the pad on his desk. "Ms. Jamison. You've been a thorn in my side for a long while. However, for this time, you can consider yourself very fortunate this young man has shouldered the responsibility." He motioned with his pen for her to go.

Hank left the room and closed the door behind her.

"Now, for you, Mr. Sawyer." The principal rose from his chair and moved to the window, speaking with his back to Tim. "You're a new student here, and come with reasonably good records. This faculty, nor I, will put up with any such bizarre behavior. He turned to face Tim. "Since this is your first time, we'll consider the matter closed, but not forgotten."

Tim breathed a sigh of relief. "Thank ya, Sir. . . . Thank ya, very, very much."

"You may go, now. But, I suggest you might be more careful with what you say in the future." The Principal walked back to his desk.

Tim headed for the door. As he opened it and was about to step through the doorway, the principal called him to a halt.

"Just a moment, Mr. Sawyer."

Tim stopped in his tracks and spun around to face his superior.

"I'm curious about something," the principal said. "You didn't happen to call her Henrietta, did you?"

A huge smile covered Tim's face as he closed the door.

* * *

The visit to the office served one benefit for Tim. It had the effect of shortening the drudge of a full class schedule. At the end of the day, most students flowed out and headed for home, while a few others hung around.

Tim and his three buddies emerged at the same time and started walking toward the shortcut home. As they reached the corner of the building, Hank sat perched on a tree stump, not too far distant, and made a motion with her head for Tim to come over.

"Ya guys go ahead. I'll catch ya later," Tim said, and ambled over to Hank.

"I don't want this to go to your head, but thanks." She got up and turned to walk away.

"Hey. Wait a minute. Ya think ya can say that and that's all there is to it?"

Hank abruptly spun to face Tim. "So, wha'da'ya want, blood?"

"No. I jest want'cha ta stop bein' so bullheaded and see that I'd like to be your friend.

"I don't need no friends."

"Dang it, you're hardheaded. Well, if'n that's the way ya want it." Tim gave a slight shrug of his shoulders and a weak wave of his hand in a 'get-lost' gesture and started to walk away.

"Sorry about your eye."

Tim stopped and turned to face Hank. "Thanks."

They paused and simply stared at each other.

"Why don't we walk home together? We can talk on the way," Tim said.

"What? And let everybody think I'm cuddlin' up'ta ya?"

"Man. Ya are somethin' else." Tim shook his head. "Look. I got my own boat. I don't need ya. But, why don't ya come by later? We could talk then."

Hank's expression changed to surprise at Tim's mention of the boat.

"I live over at the East-Side Marina. Your Mom's a friend of my Aunt. You know that. The boat's out back on a work rail. I'll be workin' on it after I get home.

"Yeah, I know where it's at. My mom's drug me over there a few times." Hank hung her head down, shrugging her shoulders as she turned to leave. "Maybe I will, . . . maybe I won't."

When Tim got home, he found Aunt Nell busy at her usual chores of cooking and baking. Harper entered the kitchen from the hallway as he came in the back door and went directly upstairs.

"Nell. Have you got a Deale phone directory?"

"Sure do. It's on top of the refrigerator."

Harper moved to get the phone book and paged though it as Tim came running through the kitchen headed for the back door.

"Whoa, slow down there, young man. Where do you think you're going so fast?"

Tim stopped abruptly at the door. "Jest goin' to the boat," Tim said, out of breath.

Aunt Nell turned from the stove and wiped her hands on her apron. "If you got homework, you just get yourself upstairs 'til it's done."

"Aw, Aunt Nell. . . . Do I have'ta. There ain't much

daylight left fer me to work on the boat. I'm a'gonna do it after dinner."

Aunt Nell caught a scrunched eyebrow look from Harper.

"Well, . . . all right. But, you best be getting it done proper.

Tim scampered out the back door.

"Ain't easy having a young'un around, is it?" Harper asked.

"Lord, a'mercy, no."

"You'll get used to it. Tim's a good boy when you come down to it."

* * *

Tim worked diligently on the aft deck swabbing with a mop. He picked up the bucket to empty it over the side onto the ground and noticed Hank watching him from near the corner of the shed. He waved his arm to welcome her aboard and she slowly walked across the yard and climbed the ladder.

Without comment, Hank moved immediately to the steps and disappeared below deck.

Tim followed.

She checked into everything as he watched.

"So, what'cha think?" Tim asked.

"It's gross with a capital 'G.'"

Tim showed disappointment. "Oh. Sorry, . . . thought ya would like it."

"No, twerp. Ya don't understand. Gross means great . . . like cold means goooood."

Tim smiled broadly.

Hank offered a high-five.

"Wait a minute. Be right back." He scampered up the steps and disappeared for several minutes.

Hank used his absence to do some more investigation of the cabin interior.

Tim suddenly reappeared in the stairwell brandishing a

pair of cokes.

"Gotta have a toast."

Hank smiled for the first time as they popped the tops and slid into separate sides of the galley booth.

"I want one thing straight up front. If you and me start hangin' round, then we'd be buddies. I ain't gonna be treated like no dumb girl."

"No Problem. . . . Ya bet." Tim took a swig of coke. "The boat would make a great clubhouse 'til we could get it in the water. And, another thing. There's a big rubber raft we could maybe fix-up, down in the shed. Wanna give me a hand?"

"Maybe. . . . I'll think about it."

"I don't know my way 'round here and ya could sure help me findin' things I be needin' fer the boat."

"I said I'd think about it." Hank slid out of the booth and went up the steps to the aft deck.

Tim followed suit.

Hank stopped at the top of the ladder. "What'cha plan to do first?"

"I've already done some, but I kind'a thought it would be best to give the cabin a real good cleanin' so's we could eat and sleep down here, if'n we got a mind to."

"Yeah. Sounds like a good idea."

"I can run a cord from the shed fer some lights and a radio and stuff and even run a hose into the fresh water tank and have runnin' water."

Hank started down the ladder. "I gotta go."

"Okay. But, ya know you're welcome, anytime."

Hank reached the ground and started running toward the roadway. "See ya around."

Tim called after her. "Hey. Ya wouldn't happen to have a tire-patch kit, would ya? I'd sure like to get that raft fixed."

"Might have."

Tim watched as Hank slowed and turned around to walk

47

backwards.

"Hey, twerp. I'll take ya up on the offer." Hank turned away and took off in a dead run.

Tim completed the mopping he had started and figured it to be near dinner time. When he got to the house, Aunt Nell was putting the final touches on the meal.

"Tim. Before you wash up I want to talk to you for a minute."

"Yes'um." He walked over and took a seat sideways on one of the chairs.

Aunt Nell carried a large bowl of salad and placed it on the table. "I want you to know I wasn't very happy when I heard about your altercation at school with Henrietta. Good Lord, child. What could have been going through your mind?"

Tim squirmed in the chair, looking downward. "Her name ain't Henrietta. It's Hank. She don't take to bein' called by her proper name."

Tim's response spurred Aunt Nell to grin. She quickly forced regaining composure. "Well. Whatever. I planned to give you a good scolding, but since I see you and Henrietta, uh, . . . Hank, have settled your differences, I guess that's what's important."

Tim looked up, showing some relief.

Aunt Nell wrung her hands in the lower part of her apron and turned to walk to the sink.

"T'won't happen agin. I promise. Can I go. now?"

Aunt Nell made several trips to the table with dishes, while continuing to talk to Tim. "Did you see Jasper, today?"

"No, Mam."

"Well. He said he patched up that old rubber boat in the work shed for you, but I'm not so sure I like the idea of it."

"Yes," Tim said, emphatically, with a pump of his fist.

"Just you mind, now. I won't have you gallivanting all over the place in that old thing, . . . and you'll be wearing a life jacket every time you even get near it."

Tim leaped to his feet and made a beeline out of the back door.

"Tim. . . . Tim! You get back here and get washed. Dinner's almost ready." Aunt Nell reached to part the curtains aside watching Tim running toward the shed. A large smile spread across her face.

* * *

Tim and Hank counted days until school would end for summer vacation, the six weeks being filled with continuous hard work on the boat. There had been many repairs made and the boat certainly in good enough shape to spend leisure time on it. Their first night of summer vacation was spent on board.

Lights glowed from the cabin windows as the voices of Mel Proctor and John Lowenstein announcing a Baltimore Oriole's baseball game become increasingly audible.

Framed through the cabin window, a black and white TV rested on the Galley counter, and two coke cans and a bag of potato chips sat on the booth table.

Tim and Hank were stretched-out on the bench seats on each side of the booth, watching the TV.

"Bet Ripken steals second," Hank said.

"No way. . . . Don't know much about the Orioles, but he ain't no base stealer.

The occasionally flickering TV picture showed Cal Ripken on first base with a big lead. The O's were down by a run in the bottom of the seventh inning with Harold Baines at the plate.

Ripken took off for second base, and Tim and Hank sat up abruptly as he is called safe at second.

"See. Told ya so."

'Awwww, . . . ya was lucky," Tim said. "Wha'da'ya really know?"

"I know we need'ta make more money if we're gonna get this boat runnin'. We done made it look halfway decent, but that don't make it float and able to go."

"Yeah, . . . but how?"

"Been thinkin'. We could catch some bull-minnows and sell 'em for bait. They's good for catchin' flounder."

Tim's smile altered to a serious expression. "How about diggin' some night-crawlers?" They both turn to sit and face each other across the table. "And, maybe we could catch crabs."

"Crabs ain't all that easy. Ya needs crab pots and a lotta fresh bait. Buyin' chicken parts costs money."

"What about usin' fish innards?"

"Where we gonna get those?" Hank asked. Can't catch big-nuff fish in the creek. They's all undersized and illegal.

We can get'em when the charter boats come in and cleans the catch. We can put 'em in Aunt Nell's freezer.

Hank expressed a big grin. "First we gotta get crab pots and build some holdin' tanks."

The TV picture displayed two Orioles rounding third base in the bottom of the ninth. They won, four to three.

* * *

As the game ended, the dark outside atmosphere held a mystic of intrigue. A freighter at anchor in Chesapeake Bay channel became alive with activity as crew men scurried about, and a huge crane hoisted a sleek cabin cruiser to hang above the water over the side of the ship. A long thin' torpedo-like capsule attached to the keel of the craft became clearly visible. Slowly, the boat, with two men aboard, was lowered into the water.

After being released, the smaller craft moved away into the night.

CHAPTER VI

The Super Snipes

An orange glow of the new day appeared over the reeds behind Aunt Nell's House. The sound of a boat motor starting indicated the early hour of fishermen getting underway.

A mother duck and her ducklings quacked unceasingly as they made their way to the creek for their morning swim.

Aboard the rail boat, the cabin doors sat open with an electric fan sitting at the top of the steps and blowing air into the lower area.

The interior remained relatively dark, brightened only by the newly rising sun. The two young adventurers were still asleep -- Tim in the fore-cabin, and Hank sprawled on the convertible bunk in the galley area.

A power boat engine back-firing stirred Hank. She abruptly sat up in the bunk, rubbed her eyes, and threw her legs over its side, slipping to a standing position. She moved to the galley sink, drew water from the faucet, and splashed her face and the back of her neck.

Drying herself with a towel, she moved to the fore-cabin and scraped her finger nails against the bottom of Tim's bare foot.

Tim reacted with a jolt, sitting upright, "Wha . . . ya crazy? What time is it, anyway?" He crawled out of the bunk.

Hank opened the refrigerator door. "It's a quarter to six.

51

The alarm didn't work." Hank took deli items from the refrigerator and began making sandwiches. "We best be gettin' a move on if we're gonna go with Jasper. Ya gotta pee? . . . I do."

"Uh, . . . yeah. Come on. We'll go inside the house. But we better get a goin'."

The sun slowly surfaced over the horizon as Jasper's boat left the Rockhold Creek channel and entered Herring Bay.

Jasper, at the helm, revved the engines and the boat lunged from the 'no-wake' restricted area to a rapid pace, throwing water behind in a large rooster-tail. Tim and Hank, clad in life-jackets, held on tightly as the boat surged forward. Moving to the stern, they felt the spray with their hands.

Eventually slowing the boat, Jasper brought it to a halt along side a crab pot marker bobbing in the water. He began with a teaching lesson. "Tim, you bring that first pot up. Hank can do the next."

Tim pulled on the line until the pot surfaced and gained a bounty of seven nice sized crabs. "Wow. This is great, Jasper."

Jasper smiled big, and moved to the next marker in line.

"Ha," Tim said. You only got six. I got seven."

"Up yours," Hank countered. "What's this supposed to be, a contest?"

"You two settle down, now. I don't need no war goin' on," Jasper said. "This is supposed to be a teachin' experience, not no competition."

"Sorry, Jasper," Tim said. "I was just jokin'."

Hank gave Tim a big smirk, and then followed it with a smile and a punch in his ribs.

On Tim's next turn, a crab got loose. "Aw, my Gawd," he hollered, scrambling to get away from the scurrying creature.

Hank and Jasper started laughing hysterically as Tim did

a jig trying to dodge the snapping escapee.

Finally regaining decorum, Jasper taught the two assistants how to capture the crab without being bit.

The work completed, Jasper headed his boat back into Deale as, exhausted, Tim and Hank rested near the stern against stacked life jackets, sound asleep.

Piloting his boat through the creek channel, Jasper waved at other captains on their way out to the bay. He passed the 'chicken-coop' marker as an osprey settled on its nest, and pulled the boat into Skipper's Pier to get gas.

Tim and Hank awoke simultaneously as the boat bumped the dock. Both sprang to their feet and assisted in tying lines to the pilings as an attendant handed Jasper the gas nozzle.

Tim and Hank scurried onto the dock.

"Gotta use the head, Jasper. We'll be right back," Tim said.

Inside the restaurant, a few patrons dined while others were seated at the bar. A rest room sign on a far wall indicated their destination as being down a darkened hallway. Tim and Hank headed in the direction of the sign and, halfway down the corridor, the door way to the men's room burst open and, impeding their way, Skull appeared.

"Aw, my Gawd," the two youths said in unison.

At first, the three stood motionless with Skull glaring at Tim and Hank. Then, the two youngsters slowly began to backup, suddenly turn, and run through the restaurant and out of the door they previously entered.

Tim and Hank continued running down the pier to Jasper's boat with Hank in the lead.

"Wha . . . Who . . . Who the hell was that?" Tim said, wheezing from being short of breath.

Gasping, Hank replied, "Skull. . . . That be Skull. . . . He's a mean one, he is."

As they reached the boat, Jasper handed the gas pump nozzle back to the Gas Attendant. "Lawdy, mercy. Y'all act like you done seen a ghost."

"Skull . . . It was Skull. . . . We done run into him comin' outta the men's room.

Tim and Hank jumped down into the boat.

"I'd rather pee my pants than face that monster." Tim said.

Hank eagerly agreed. "Me, too. Gawd, me, too."

Jasper struggled to suppress a grin. "Lawdy. . . . Sure understand that. Rumor has it he's done away with a few good men in his past."

Tim practically begged Jasper. "Cain't we get outta here?"

Unable to restrain himself any longer, Jasper broke into a big smile followed by a chuckle. "Untie them lines and we be gone."

Tim and Hank couldn't get them untied fast enough. They pushed the boat from the dock and stood at the stern staring at Skull striding down Skipper's Pier toward the Gas Dock and his own small boat.

Shortly arriving at the marina, Jasper backed into his slip. Tim and Hank tied the lines to the pier and helped Jasper unload the baskets of crabs.

"You young'uns have sure been a big help. Y'all take on off, now. I can take care of the rest.

"Thanks, Jasper. We still gotta pee real bad," Hank said.

Jasper busted out laughing and waved a get-going gesture as Tim and Hank sped down the pier and ran across the backyard to Aunt Nell's house.

Tim headed straight for the back door as Hank came to a halt. "Ain't ya comin' in?"

"I gotta get home. Promised my mom I'd do some chores this afternoon. I can hold it 'til I get there." Hank spun on her heels and began to trot away, then suddenly stopped and turned as Tim was halfway through the back door. "Hey, twerp. . . . I almost forgot."

Tim stopped in the doorway as Hank took a few steps

towards him.

"Smudge told me there's a bunch of things we could use over on the scrap-heap at Tracy's Boat Yard."

"Oh, yeah," Tim said. "But, I really gotta pee."

"All right . . . hold your horses just a minute. This is important. He said there was an old fishin' net, a crab pot, and a bunch of neat things. If we're gonna run a crab trot-line we could sure use the cork floats off the net. But, there's a hitch."

"What's that?"

"We gotta sneak in and get it. They don't like kids snoopin' round." Hank turned to leave. "Anyway, we'll talk about it later. See ya."

Tim started to go inside of the house and suddenly stopped and called out to Hank, "What about tonight?"

Hank called back. "Did ya get the raft fixed, again?"

"Yeah. Like new."

"I'll be back real late."

* * *

Near midnight, the moon shined brightly and the sounds of crickets and night birds abounded. Tim's rubber raft rested in the water, tied to a piling near the rail boat.

At the house, Tim's window was dark as gravel pellets bounced off of it. Hank stood below looking up and tossing small pieces of gravel.

Pulling the window curtains aside, Tim stuck his head through the opening. "Okay, . . . okay. I'll be right there," he said, in a loud whisper.

Moments later Tim quietly exited the rear door and he and Hank snuck across the yard toward the Marina and climbed into the raft.

Pushing the small craft from the shore, soft sounds of oars drawing through the dark water represented the only interruption to the silence of the night. They quietly paddle their way down Rockhold Creek on their way to Tracy's Landing Boatyard.

"Ya think Smudge knows what he's talkin' about?" Hank asked, in almost a whisper.

"Reckon so. Least, he swore he'd eat a grub worm if'n he'd be wrong."

Hank giggled. "That'd be worth seein'."

"I ain't got no idea where Tracy's Landing Boatyard is."

"Next to Tracy's Landing Marina, dumb ass." Hank giggled some more. "Don't sweat it. I do."

The earlier well lit night slowly became darker due to the moon moving behind clouds in a partially covered sky. Light reflected from the shoreline to serve as a navigational aid to their destination.

"That's it, over there," Hank said, in a whisper as they paddled toward shore and got out of their raft. The landing area was a dirt and gravel beach cluttered with twisted vines and underbrush.

Dragging their small craft away from the water, a spotlight swept near their position as the low purr of motors were first heard from an oncoming water craft.

"Aw, shit. . . . Scoot," Hank said, a bit louder than intended.

The two scrambled through the underbrush until reaching a disposal pile offering limited seclusion -- a chain link fence separated them from the boatyard.

The craft arrived at the boatyard. Tim and Hank watched as the small cruiser entered a man-made channel stopping just short of a large enclosed boat shed. Two occupants climbed ashore.

Tim and Hank overheard the ensuing conversation.

"What the hell's goin' on?" the second mate said, gruffly.

The first mate replied, "Damn it. George was supposed to be here. He's probably drunk and sleepin' it off."

"Well, I don't like it. I'm gettin' fed up with takin' all the risks."

"Shut up, you idiot. You want to wake the world. "I'm

gettin' tired of hearin' your belly-achin'. You make good money for what you're doin'. Wait here. I'll be right back." The first mate finished tying a line and moved to a side shed door and entered it.

* * *

Through the dimly lit interior, the first mate crossed the area to where George sat sleeping -- his feet propped on his desk -- a bottle of booze and a glass on the floor beside his chair.

The first mate raised his foot and shoved the chair in a backward motion, tipping it over.

George sprawled on the floor. "Wha . . . What'd ya do dat for?" he asked, in a stupor.

"Get your ass up and open the door."

George struggled to his feet, responding to the first mate's demand. The shed's doors rolled upward as the second mate jumped into the boat and guided it by hand along the sides of the concrete wall of the channel into the building.

The large shed door rolled back into place and the first mate hurried back through the side door, closing it with a bang.

* * *

Tim and Hank remained huddled in their place.

"Wha'da'ya make of that?" Hank whispered.

"I don't know, but somethin' ain't right. Wha'da'ya think?"

"Let's take a peek in the window and find out." Hank tugged at Tim's sleeve as she started to move toward the fence.

"Ya, nuts? . . . Let's get what we came fer and get outta here."

"Okay, chicken. Start cuttin' off the floats from the net. I'll be right back."

"Aw, shit. . . ."

Hank crept along the fence, finding an opening large

57

enough for her to squeeze through. She silently snuck toward the side of the huge shed to a window and placed cinder blocks sitting nearby in a manner to be able to stand on them to see inside.

The interior of the building is brightly lit and Hank watched as a huge boat-lift lifted the newly arrived craft from the water. As it cleared the bulkhead, a long slim torpedo-like structure mounted on the keel became clearly visible. Immediately, the crane swings the boat to the side s the where the First Mate and Second Mate begin removing the capsule.

A large dog appeared and started barking at Hanks window.

George descended the boat-lift's ladder. "Shut up, Killer. Go lay down," he gruffly shouted, while joining the other two and giving assistance to their chore.

Ignoring George's command, Killer continued his barking.

The First Mate became increasingly disturbed. "What the hell's wrong with him? Go check it out."

"It's probably that damn raccoon that hangs around outside. Killer. I said shut up," he again shouted.

"I said go check it out, Damn it," First Mate demanded.

* * *

Hank watched long enough to see George putting a leash on the dog, then scurried from her perch and rushed in a crouch across the distance, finally squeezing back through the fence opening.

Hank reached Tim as he placed an armful of floats into the raft. She grabbed hold of one side of the raft and started dragging it toward the water. "Let's get the hell outta here."

"What happened?"

"Just shut up and move."

Tim grasped the other side of the raft, helping to get it quickly back into the water. They both jumped into the small craft and used the oars to propel them as quietly as possible into the dark waters.

Ashore, Killer's barking continued as they watched George and the dog roaming around the area they had just left.

CHAPTER VII

Church Bells Ring

The congregation stood and began singing the closing hymn. Hank took a glance at Tim and shook her head in an 'I'm glad it's over' gesture.

As the hymn finished, the Pastor spoke. "Before we have the benediction, there's a matter I'd like to bring to your attention. He moved from behind the pulpit and stopped at the top of the altar steps and motioned with his hand to a lady sitting in the first pew.

As an elderly lady rose and moved to join the Pastor, he addressed the congregation. "I'd like to introduce Mrs. Kathleen Ellen Catwell, a noted author and historian."

The Pastor's guest, dressed in a light gray women's business suit, moved to stand before the microphone. "Thank you, Reverend," she said, nodding to the Pastor and, then, responding to her audience. "And, thank you for the opportunity to bring this matter before you." She paused slightly. "Today's sermon is very fitting to my story.

Tim squirmed in his seat, totally disinterested and glanced in Hank's direction. They both visually expressed similar attitudes of wanting to get church over with.

"As Daniel proved his bravery in the den, over many ages, there have been numerous heroes counted in the pages of history. There have also been endless gallant acts going unnoticed, or dismissed.

Ms. Catwell stared in Tim's direction.

Tim became uneasy uneasily at eye contact and looked away, maintaining a lack of interest in it all.

Hank continued to appear equally disinterested and yawned.

"A few months ago, I had been in Richmond for a seminar. Deciding to take a bus for the short distance home, I had the opportunity to meet a fine young man seated next to me."

Tim looked shocked; as if he'd been hit with a bucket of cold water.

Aunt Nell patted him on the leg, while exposing a proud smile and a glistening of tearing eyes.

"We befriended each other for those short few minutes before an accident occurred. My young friend had went to the rear to wash his hands and, while in the rest room, the bus careened from the highway into a deep crevice.

Tim's face altered rapidly from looks of disbelief to complete embarrassment -- his mouth agape.

"I was knocked unconscious. This youth was credited with saving my life." She paused for a moment. "Until recently, I didn't even know his name. He never knew mine. Through records at the hospital, I found the needed information." She stepped from behind the pulpit and motioned for Tim to join her on the podium. "May I present to you my friend, and my hero, Tim Sawyer."

The congregation buzzed with conversation, staring in Tim's direction. Tim looked like he wanted to hide, as Aunt Nell prodded him to rise and go forward.

Tim reluctantly struggled to his feet and slowly made his way toward the front of the church.

The congregation rose with thunderous applause and cheers.

Hank sat with a dumbfounded expression, glaring at Tim as he arrived on the podium.

"Right over here." Mrs. Catwell motioned Tim to her, and shook his hand.

"Hi . . . ," Tim meekly muttered.

"Hello. It's wonderful to see you, again.

Mrs. Catwell subtly removed an envelop from her suit coat pocket. "Money certainly shouldn't be the most important thing in our lives, but sometimes it may be the only way to show the true appreciation one may have." She opened the envelope. "Tim. On behalf of myself, and my family, I'd like to present you with three checks, each for one thousand dollars."

Tim gulped and expressed a shocked grin.

"The first is to be used to establish a trust fund for your further education. The second, a donation to your church in your name." Mrs. Catwell beamed with a huge smile. "And last, but certainly not least, one is made out to you to buy whatever you desire." She handed the checks to Tim and stepped forward giving him a big hug. The applause was ear-shattering.

* * *

Church Bells rang as parishioners surrounded and lauded Tim with congratulations, as he exited the front doors. He spotted Hank standing aside, grinning from ear-to-ear.

Totally embarrassed, Tim tried to make his way through the many admirers, and then away from the crowd in the direction of Hank. As he reached her, they gave each other the 'high-five;' grabbed each other in their arms; began to spin, and jump up and down, while laughing loudly.

Suddenly, they stopped, looked at each other, and broke from their embrace -- both reflecting embarrassment at having made intimate contact.

Hank quickly moved backwards. "Don't cha think you're somethin'."

Tim smiled from ear-to-ear. "I think we're a'gonna buy Jasper's rowboat and motor. That's what I think."

Hank threw a fake punch in his direction and turned, trotting away--Tim following behind.

* * *

Tim and Hank brought their boat to a halt near Buoy One just off from Holland Point, and dropped anchor, hurrying to bait their lines and cast them overboard.

"Oh, wow. I got one already," Hank said with great excitement.

"Me, too." Tim was all smiles.

Within about a half-hour, they boated over a dozen nice sized Norfolk spot. "Holy cow," Hank hollered, as her pole bent well over, and struggled to reel in her catch.

"Don't lose it," shouted Tim. "Don't lose it."

Hank finally got the huge flounder in the boat. "I never thought these things would bite on a worm. Must've been really hungry," she said, standing in the middle of the boat and holding the fish over her head. "Ya ain't caught one like this. She's a beaut, . . . ain't she?

Tim ignored her as she stuck her tongue out at him, laughing loudly. Tim finally altered his faked disinterest and joined in the levity.

Totally distracted by the fun, neither paid attention to the oncoming sleek boat as it sped past and nearby them. It seemed to appear out of nowhere and rocked their boat violently in its wake. Hank lost her balance and nearly thrown overboard before Tim grabbed her just in time. However, in the process, she lost her prize fish.

"Dern them crazies," she said screaming. . . . Just dern them!"

"Holy crap. Do ya know who . . . what that be? That be the weird boat we saw the other night at Tracy's Landing."

Still in a rage, Hank agreed. "You're right. It was. You're dern sure dern right."

They watched for a few seconds as the speedy craft is distancing itself toward the Eastern Shore.

"Come on. Let's follow 'em. See where the hell there goin," Tim said.

"They're too fast for us. We'd never catch 'em."

"We can follow their wake if'n we hurry."

Hank quickly hauled in the anchor as Tim pulled the outboard motor to a roar. The small craft spun in the water and headed in an Eastward direction following the distancing speedster.

Near the center of the Bay, Tim slowed their boat to a steady pace as they watched their prey sidle-up to a freighter anchored in the shipping channel.

"Hey. Why don't we stop here and throw our lines over so's they's think we're fishin? We could watch and see what they's doin," Tim suggested.

"We can't. The water round here's about a hundred or more feet deep. They'd know we was just bein' nosy. Ya just don't go bait fishin' this far out."

Tim's expression suddenly altered to that of great concern on learning the depth of the water, and stared over the side of the boat as if trying to confirm Hank's statement. He turned to confront Hank. "Well, they's gonna think somethin, anyway, if'n we jest turn around and skedaddle right back."

"You're probably right. Let's keep goin' right on by. We'll act like we're headed over to the Eastern Shore.

Yeah, . . . good idea. They don't know if'n we're from over there, or not." Tim accelerated the motor to a faster pace.

As they passed far astern of the huge ship, their last glimpse afforded a view of the smaller craft being hoisted aboard the freighter by a huge crane. The torpedo-like capsule was missing from beneath.

Tim opened the throttle even further and their small craft surged forward carrying them farther away from their home port.

Daylight quickly lost its glow as heavy blackening clouds covered the south-western skies in the distance. The sea quickly began to become more choppy, and smaller craft could be seen rushing toward the nearest shoreline.

As they approached the Eastern Shore, the bow of their

boat beat into the waves as a heavy spray pounded both Tim and Hank. Although the shore was visible, the bobbing of the craft made it difficult to hold a steady course. They had no idea where they were.

* * *

A roar of thunder resounded as lightning flashed through the kitchen windows. Aunt Nell stood at the sink cleaning dishes after baking. Harper sat at the table with a cup of coffee and reading the newspaper. The wall clock read eight thirty-five p.m.

"Lord a'mercy. That sure is a storm a'comin'. . . . I sure hope the children will be okay." Aunt Nell turned, wiping her hands in her apron.

Harper looked up from his paper and smiled. "You fret too much. They'll be fine on that old boat. It'd take Noah's flood to get it off that rail."

Aunt Nell carried a fresh cup of coffee to the table in one hand and the pot in the other to refill Harper's cup. "I guess I'm just a worry-wart old maid. It's just hard to adjust to havin' young'un around when you're at my age." She took a seat across from Harper.

"You're doin' a great job with the boy, but he's growin' up and needs his space." If you're really concerned, I'll go down to the Marina and check them out.

I'm being foolish. . . . No, it's raining too hard and I reckon they'd be high-tailin' it up here if they were scared.

* * *

The harsh winds had eased and the heavy rains subsided to a steady drizzle. The ominous clouds were breaking with small patches of clear darkened sky becoming visible with an occasional embrace of the full moon.

Tim and Hank huddled in the bottom of their boat which is sitting deep among the bulrushes. Tim unrolled the surviving sleeping bag to shelter them both from the chill. Most of their gear had been lost in the storm.

"Ya all right?" Tim asked, his teeth chattering.

66

Hank shivered. "Yea . . . yeah. Just cold."

"We gotta be real dumb. Where do ya think we are?"

"I don't know. . . . Got no idea how far we could'a gone, North or South. It all depends on which way the sea was taken us." Hank shivered and snuggled closer to Tim under the sleeping bag.

"Ya scared?"

"Who, . . . me?" Hank asked indignantly. . . . Well, maybe a little bit."

"Me, too," Tim said, muttering his reply.

They squirmed and cuddled even closer as Tim said, "Reckon we best wait 'til morning to do anything.

"Yeah. We'll probably have to get out and pull this thing through these reeds by hand. . . . I know the prop's all fouled up. I just hope it ain't bent. Wouldn't do no good in this stuff, anyway."

"Aw, crap. . . . I jest thought. What if Aunt Nell finds out we ain't on the rail boat?"

"Aaaahhh, she ain't gonna know. Least, not tonight, I bet. No doubt the storm hit home no different than it did here. She'll just figure we're warm and cozy watchin' television, or somethin'. I reckon we ought'a try and . . ."

Hank was rudely interrupted by a sudden jolt of their rowboat. The huge shadowy upper torso of a figure had grabbed hold of the anchor rope dangling over the bow, and wades through the weeds pulling their boat behind him.

Terrified and whispered, Hank said, "Aw, God, we're goners. Aw, shit, Tim. What we gonna do? It's Skull."

"Hell . . . dang. Danged if I know. What can we do?" Tim replied, with equal fright apparent in his whispered voice.

Tim and Hank dared to take a peek. The other side of the reed area opened into a lagoon bordered by tall trees on three sides. A break in the clouds afforded the moonlight to provide a dim view of the surroundings.

On the far end of the lagoon rested a huge sailboat with

its bow beached on the shore. A flickering light could be seen emanating from its lower cabin portholes.

Skull drug their boat to the shore and beached it in the sand. He gruffly motioned with his arm, with an accompanying grunt, for Tim and Hank to get out of the boat. Hesitantly, they followed his command.

As they reached ground, Skull grabbed each of them by the back of their life-jackets and roughly ushered them toward the sailboat.

A tall silhouetted figure of a man, hovered above them, standing on the bow of his craft.

Skull pushed the two toward a ladder leaning against the stern of the sailboat and they climbed upwards with the giant of a man close behind.

The interior of the sailboat proved warm and cozy, but somewhat cluttered with books and papers strewn about. It showed signs of having been occupied for a good period of time. A typewriter sat on the galley table with a sheet of paper extended above its carriage.

A kerosene lamp provided lighting that flicked off the white painted interior turned cream from wear and dust.

A tall lanky man of late middle-age with a long mingled grey beard, wearing a dark captain's jacket and hat with gold braid, motioned for Tim and Hank to take a seat on a nearby vinyl covered bunk. He sat across from them in a high-backed overstuffed chair, placing a large bowled pipe between his teeth and lighting it with a match.

Skull returned from a fore-cabin with a couple of blankets, and handed them to Tim and Hank.

"You best be gettin' outta them wet clothes.

Tim and Hank responded immediately, removing the life-jackets and wrapping themselves in the blankets before removing the rest. Skull stood looming in the way of any thoughts of escape, blocking access to the upper deck.

"If my old friend, here, hadn't been out nosyin' around he wouldn't have heard your boat engine gettin' tangled up in those reeds." He paused to take a long slow drag from his pipe. You would have doubt caught pneumonia 'fore the night was over." He paused to take another puff. "What in tarnation are you two young'uns doin' out on the Bay on a night like this?

Tim and Hank sheepishly looked downward, reluctant to meet his gaze.

Tim stammered. "Well, . . . I . . . We . . .

"Heave to, boy. The truth boy. I want the truth, mind you.

"I'm a'tryin', sir. But . . ."

"No need to be afraid, boy. No need to be afraid."

"Yes, sir. But . . ."

"What be your names?"

"I'm Tim . . . Tim Sawyer, sir. This is my friend, Hank."

"Humphhh. . . . What kind'a name is Hank for a girl. . . . Humphhh."

In defiance, Hank spoke. "I don't give a . . ."

Tim immediately sensed Hank's tenderness to the subject and poked her in the ribs interrupting her response.

A tea kettle on the stove began to whistle and Skull rose his chair and moved to the galley.

"We could all use some warmin' up, don't you think?"

"Yes, sir," Hank and Tim replied in unison.

Skull fixes each a mug and distributes them amongst all present and returned to take his seat.

If ya don't mind, sir. Could I ask who ya might be?

They're benefactor smiled for the first time. "Well, . . . I reckon you've a right to know." He paused a moment to sip from his cup. "My friend who found you is Skull. What his real name is . . . don't know . . . and, don't really care. He don't talk none. . . . Don't know why . . . and, really don't care. You get to know him and he's got a way of lettin' you know what he wants or what he thinks."

Skull stepped forward and offered his hand to Tim and Hank. Their faces reflected a marvel at the gentleness of his handshake.

"As for me, I'm Captain James. Captain James Sawyer, that is . . . Humphhh."

Tim appeared stunned, his mouth agape. "You're . . . . Holy cow! You're my Uncle . . ."

Appearing startled, Captain James squirmed in his seat.

"Humphhh. . . . What? What's all this nonsense, you say?"

"When ya said your name, I recognized ya from your pictures at home. You're beard's longer. But, you're my Uncle James. That's fer sure."

"You don't know what you're talkin' about, boy. The storm must'a made you loony."

"Oh, no sir. You're my Aunt Nell's brother, you are, . . . and my Uncle, too."

Captain James appeared shocked.

Hank appeared totally dumbfounded, staring at the both of them.

Skull simply let out a snort . . .

* * *

Skull finished loading his boat, and also had Tim and Hank's boat ready to leave.

Tim, Hank and Captain James debark the sailboat and, as they reached the ground, walked toward the two small crafts.

"Now, both of you be rememberin' what I told you last night. Ain't none to know about you seein' me. Especially your Aunt Nell. . . . Humphhh. Oh, well, if you got to tell someone, . . . just let Jasper know. He can keep a good secret. But, not another soul, mind you.

"Oh, we won't, sir. We promise with our lives," Tim said as a sincere vow.

Hank readily shook her head in positive agreement.

"Well, I appreciate that, but it might be stretchin' things a bit far." He laughed. "Another thing. You both be better forgettin' about what you saw. Those people could be up to

70

somethin bad, . . . really bad. Best you be mindin' your own business.

"Yes, sir," Tim meekly agreed.

Arriving at the boats, Tim and Hank got in theirs.

"You just follow Skull outta here and back home cross the Bay. If you're lucky, you'll get back 'fore someone finds you've been missin'. And, remember . . . give Skull a note from time to time. He'll bring it to me." Captain James pulled his pipe from his jacket pocket and placed it between his teeth. "And, I don't want you two young'uns tryin' to cross that bay in that little boat, again. . . . You hear me? Humphhh. . . . An, put them life-jackets on, right now."

Tim and Hank responded in unison. "Yes, sir."

Captain James pushed their boat off of the beach as Skull did the same with his own. He waded in the water and climbed aboard. "Captain . . . Uncle James. It be sure great seein' ya. And, thanks fer everythin'," Tim called out, just before he pulled the motor to life.

Captain James' facade of indifference became shattered as his eyes showed a slight watering. He struggled to smile. "You be a Sawyer, all right. Just like your old ancestor, Tom. Runs in the family, you know. Just you be keepin' that need to be explorin' in check." He waved. "Get along, now. Time's wastin'."

Skull steered his boat through a narrow opening in the reeds and into the Bay. Hank and Tim followed closely.

CHAPTER VIII

Believe It or Not

Jasper was on the dock approaching his slip when he waved at Skull passing his pier -- Tim and Hank not far behind. Skull continued further up the creek, motioning a so-long to the two young wayfarers as they moved their boat into shore next to the rail boat.

As soon as they secured the boat, Tim and Hank rushed up the dock to confront Jasper.

"Jasper. . . . Oh, Gawd, Jasper. Ya jest ain't gonna believe this."

"God, no, Jasper, . . . ya can't believe it."

Jasper smiled and waved his hands in a quieting manner. "Whoa, now. . . . What I believe is I just seen the two of you wavin' back and forth with Skull, but I ain't gonna get a chance to believe anythin' else if I don't get a chance to hear it. Let's go aboard the big boat so's we's can talk."

Tim, Hank and Jasper are all seated in the galley area booth.

Jasper initiated the conversation. "What is yous two doin' out so early in the mornin'. And, where's yous been? Yous two been out all night, I figure. Tim, don't yous know what Nell would do if she knew it?"

Tim showed slight shame, but brightened quickly. "Jasper, that's what we been tryin' to tell ya. We got caught out in the storm yesterday evenin' and wound up on the Eastern Shore. Capt, . . . Uncle James is alive."

Jasper's eyes got as big as saucers.

"Yeah, and I'll vouch for it," Hank added.

Before Jasper could comment, Tim continued. "We got washed up in some thick reeds and wound up findin' Uncle James."

"And, it was Skull that pulled us outta them reeds into a big lagoon that nobody knows is there. Ol' Skull is a pretty good guy after all," Hank said.

Still showing some surprise and possible doubt, Jasper said, "I could'a told yous that."

"And Uncle James told us ya are the only one we could tell. No one else can find out. Ya promise."

"Yeah, . . . I'll keep it a secret. Sure sounds like you's Uncle James." Jasper smiled. "Did he tells ya what happened and whys he's there?"

Tim responded excitedly. "You bet he did. He be a'comin' back from Norfolk and got caught in a big storm and washed ashore just likes we did. Gawd must'a guided us there last night, I figure. After his boat got stuck, he said he liked it there and decided to stay and write a book. Skull be with him when it happened and has been a'usin' the sailboat's dingy to travel back and forth to get supplies for Uncle James."

Jasper shook his head. "Don't get me wrong, I believes yous. Just it's surprisin' and some real good news." He reached across the table and gave Tim's head a good rub.

Tim and Hank completed their tale of the rest of the evening.

"I know it sounds like a tall-story, but like Uncle James made me promise, it's the truth."

"We swear it is, Jasper."

"Well, I figured the old buzzard was still 'round somewhere. . . . Just didn't know where." Jasper slid out of his seat. "Yous two gots to excuse me. I gotta get the boat runnin' to work my line." Jasper turned to leave. "If yous want, yous can go with me."

Tim and Hank look questionably at each other.

"Go ahead and ask him, Tim."

Jasper stopped in his tracks and turned to face them. "Ask what?"

"I wanna get this boat off'n the rail. . . . I wanna get it a'runnin'. . . . Ya know I still got money left from the gift I got. Would ya help us get her in the water?"

"Boy, . . . you ain't got no idea what yous askin'. Them engines ain't been run in ages. It's likely they's done froze up. On tops of that, the bottom needs sandin' and paintin'. Even then, it'd take days in the water, pumpin' out, for the hull to swell together. Besides, what's yous Aunt Nell gonna say?" Jasper turned and climbed the steps to the bridge.

Hank and Tim followed.

"Why does she gotta know?"

Jasper stopped abruptly and turned to face Hank.

"Just you hold up young lady. I'm nots about to do nothin' agin her wishes."

Hank expressed an 'oops, that was a mistake' look.

"Won't ya put in a good word fer us?" Tim implored.

"Young'un. It ain't about that. It's about what's good for yous. If'n yous got ideas about confrontin' the bay so's yous can make trips to see Captain James, this old boat's most likely more than you can handle. I sees how much it meant meetin' you's uncle, . . . but he'd want me to do no different, I'm sure."

"Sorry, Jasper. But, Uncle James would figure I wouldn't give up tryin, neither."

Jasper expressed a big smile. "Yous right about that. . . . Yous sure right. That's I can't deny." He started to leave, but stopped and changed his tact. "I'll mention somethin' to Nell. And, it sho wouldn't hurt for youse to get Maggie on your side, too. . . . But, mind you, I'm gonna tell Nell yous promise not to take her outta the slip alone. You hear?"

* * *

Tim and Hank handled the next several days using great tact and effort to achieve their goal.

Tim bent over backwards to be of help to his Aunt. He and Hank gathered fresh cut flowers, some from nearby neighbor's gardens, and carried them to see Aunt Maggie. After that, they visited Smudge, Frog and Smoke as they were playing a baseball game at the school's athletic field -- all leading to a direct confrontation with Aunt Nell, who had been coerced into inviting Hank for dinner.

The meal over, and the boarders back in their rooms, Tim bided his time cautiously. "Is there anythin' we can do, Aunt Nell?"

Nell returned to the table with a fresh cup of coffee and sat down. "No need to keep butterin' me up, Tim. I know what you really want."

Tim and Hank both exhibit a sullen expression.

"I know you've been gettin' Jasper and Maggie on your side. They've both been after me." From a stone-face, she smiles broadly. "Cheer up. I haven't said no."

The two youngster's faces slightly lit up.

"I've been doin' a lot of thinkin' about it. I decided, if you two young'uns have the spunk to do it, you can. Least it'll keep you occupied and outta trouble."

Tim and Hank jumped from their seats cheering and giving each other a 'high-five.'

* * *

Occupied proved to be an understatement. The ensuing weeks were spent entirely on the project of restoration. Many trips were made to the local marine store buying bottom paint and other materials, usually carting them home in a wheelbarrow.

All of Tim's friends joined in to help with the rail boat, including Jasper working on the engines.

* * *

Aunt Nell broke a large bottle filled with Koolaid on the bow with all the gang present and cheering, as Jasper manned the helm. Tim and Hank sat on the bow.

Frog released the pulley, allowing the rail boat to slide backwards into the water. Everybody cheered even louder and frantically waved.

* * *

The rail boat rested in its slip as lights from inside reflected across the water. The humming sound of the bilge pump breaking the silence of the evening.

Inside, Tim and Hank sat in the galley area across from each other, paying strained attention to the TV flickering due to the incessant drone and interference of the bilge pump.

"It's been a'runnin' fer most a week, now. Won't that thing ever stop." Tim moaned.

"Takes time, Jasper says."

"I know. . . . I know. But, I cain't sleep another night with that damn thing goin' all the time."

Hank returned a big grin and slipped off the bench seat to go to the refrigerator and, suddenly, the bilge pump's drone stopped.

Aw, Gawd, . . . it's done burned out.

Hank dropped to her knees and gazed into the open bilge area. "No it ain't. It done cut-off automatic cause there ain't enough water comin' in to pump.

Tim leaped from his seat, dropping to his knees across from Hank. After staring into the hole, the two raise up and give each other a 'high-five.'

* * *

Tim and Hank climbed off the rail boat, meeting Jasper on the pier.

"Where you two young'uns headed?"

"We're starvin'. Gonna get somethin' to eat," Tim said.

The three started walking together up the pier toward the shore.

"I noticed this mornin' yous bilge pump done cut off. That's a good sign."

They walked a little further.

"Bet yous never had one of those great big fat and juicy hamburger-deluxes from over Happy Harbor?"

"Wow. You're makin' my belly groan," Hank said.

"Tell you what. I got a little job on a boat over dere at the marina. Why don't I just treat yous both to one of 'em?"

"Yes!" With a pump of their fists.

Jasper got into the driver's seat as Tim and Hank scurried into the back of his pickup truck. They drove slowly down the dirt road past Aunt Nell's house, pausing for a line of ducks to cross their path.

* * *

Jasper pulled into the parking lot and came to a halt. He exited his side, as Tim and Hank jumped out of the back. The three crossed the road and walked toward the restaurant.

"Yous two go in and order me one, too, with an ice tea. I'm gonna run on down and check out the boat. I'll be with you young'un in a few minutes."

Jasper took off in one direction around the restaurant exterior towards the restaurant docks as Tim and Hank headed inside. They entered the bar area of the restaurant, which was dark and dingy -- the three-sided near oval bar surrounded with customers, about half of them being bikers in leathers and jeans.

Seeing an opening to the main restaurant and a brighter room, they headed for it.

Once inside the dining area, three of the walls were covered with glass windows allowing much light from outside. They scanned the room and opted on an open table near the back entrance and sat down. Watching out of the window next to them, they saw Jasper getting off a large boat at the far end of the pier, and begin to walk toward the restaurant.

A waitress arrived. "Are you ready to order?"

Not expecting her arrival, Tim and Hank jumped and quickly turned around to respond.

Hank and Tim both spoke simultaneously. "Yeah, . . . I want . . ."

The Waitress interrupted, smiling, "One at a time, please."

Hank looked at Tim and shrugged her shoulders.

"Three hamburger-deluxes, two root beers, and an iced tea, please," Tim said, breaking the standoff. "Tim pointed in the direction of Jasper. "The extra one's fer him out there. He'll be here in a minute."

"We don't have root beer. Will cokes be okay?" Their waitress smiled even broader.

Tim and Hank nodded their approval.

As the Waitress retreats, Tim and Hank noticed the list of trivia questions adorning their place mats.

"Know any of the answers?" Hank asked.

"Hummm. . . . Nope. Wait, here's one. Who's picture's on the thousand dollar bill?"

Hank glanced at Tim and snickered. "How should I know? I ain't never seen one. If I did, I'd spend it so fast I wouldn't have time to look at any old picture."

Jasper entered from a rear entrance and approached. "Youse ordered, yet?"

"A few minutes ago," Tim responded.

Jasper pulled a twenty dollar bill out of his pocket. "I gotta run up the road to the parts store and the bank 'fore it closes. Youse get mine to go. I won't be too long." Jasper laid the money on the table and departed.

Hank squirmed in her seat. "Man. I don't wanna sit in this
place by ourselves."

"Me, either. Let's get it all to go."

Tim spotted their waitress on the other side of the restaurant and went to let her know of the change of plans, then returned to his seat.

The two sat quietly watching out of the windows at the activity on the creek just behind the restaurant.

"Here you go." The Waitress handed them two relatively large paper bags. "Be careful of this one. Keep it upright so you don't spill the drinks."

Tim handed her the money and followed her to the cashier counter as Hank walked out through the rear door onto the deck.

Hank sat sideways on an outside bench table seat as Tim arrived, exiting the restaurant rear door. She got up to meet him and the two walked down the long pier running parallel to the shore, almost to its end. Jasper's toolbox rested on a finger-pier separating two slips--one empty and the other occupied by a large boat. Its aft-deck canvas tent-cover had been unzipped.

"Wha'da'ya think, Hank?"

"Let's board her. He won't mind."

CHAPTER IX

To Be; Or not to Be

They carefully climbed aboard through the tent-cover opening, placed the bags on the deck, and scanned the area.

The aft area was quite large, with dark blue covered deck chairs and a full glass wall of sliding doors leading to a salon cabin. A shiny chrome ladder allowing access to the flying-bridge was to one side.

Hank almost swooned. "Wow. I ain't never been on a boat this big, . . . or this nice.

"Me, either."

Hank moved toward the sliding doors covered with drapes blocking their view. "Let's take a gander inside."

"I don't know. Jasper might get mad if'n we go nosyin round." Tim's concern was sincere.

"Aw, come on, chicken. He ain't gonna care." She tried to slide open the doors, but found them locked. "Nuts. . . . Double nuts." She moved to the bottom of the ladder, paused while looking up, then ascended the steps until disappearing from view.

Tim heard a shuffling sound from above. "Man. Ya gonna get us in a whole bunch of trouble."

"Hey, Twerp. Get the bags. It's great up here. . . . It's like ya can almost see forever."

Tim grabbed the bags and removed a sandwich and Jasper's tea, sitting them on his toolbox, then handed them up to Hank, and climbed the steps.

81

As Tim arrived on the flying-bridge, Hank, stood holding the bags of lunch at the ship's helm.

The flying-bridge was entirely covered with canvas and the windshield and sides offered a panoramic view through smoke tinted windows, dulling the sun's penetration. Two plush leather helm seats adorned the front -- the dash full of gauges, meters and instruments. Everything inside sparkled and gleamed.

Their panoramic view scan through the windows, ended with a bay-built fishing boat arriving at the marina and maneuvering to back into the open slip next to them.

Tim and Hank sat side-by-side in the two helm seats munching on their sandwiches.

"Boy. This hamburger's sure good," Tim said, wiping his mouth with his shirt tail.

Hank nodded affirmatively with her mouth totally full.

The sound of the fishing boat's engine docking next to them increased to a loud roar.

Tim stared out of the window at the incoming craft and suddenly ducked down below the dash board. "Get down. Quick."

Hank looked at him like he'd gone crazy. "What the hell ya doin?"

"Them guys, . . . Them guys in the boat comin' in . . ." Tim kept jabbing his hand and finger, pointing over his shoulder, at the window near his side. "It's them. The ones from Tracy's."

Hank rose and leaned over to get a better look. "You're right."

"Get down, damn it."

Hank started laughing loudly. "They cain't see us with these windows. . . . And, they cain't hear us with that motor.

"Oh. I knew that. I was just jokin'."

As the craft came to a halt in the slip, four men were on board. Tim recognized two of them as George and the Second Mate, who was tying up to the dock, as the other two unknowns gathered their paraphernalia. All appeared drunk except Second Mate.

The two men who were strangers to Tim and Hank, put the top back on a large ice chest full of fish, and while saying farewells, carried it from the boat and down the pier to a spur and continued toward the shore.

Tim and Hank, even though they couldn't be seen, knelt on their knees at the rear corner of the flying-bridge peeking over the window's edge, watching the two below. Tim continued to chew on the last part of his sandwich and munching potato chips.

Second Mate shut the engines down and moved to the rear of the craft and began dipping creek water in a bucket and splashing it over the aft deck of the Fishing Boat. Drunken George struggled making his way along the gunnel from the bow to the aft deck.

"You idiot. Be careful. . . . You're gonna fall."

George almost lost his balance. "Who, me? . . . Ol' sure foot, that's me. I . . . Oooops," he said in a slurred voice.

George barely managed to throw his weight sideways before falling into the water, landing on the aft deck, instead. When his feet hit the deck, they slipped from under him on the watery surface and wound up flat on his butt. He groaned and rolled to his hands and knees.

Second Mate walked over and helped him up. "God. Why the hell Cash keeps you on, I'll never understand. Just get your damn things together and go home and get sober."

George began to spin slowly in a dancing fashion while singing a lilting tune. "Cash . . . Oh, Mr. Cash . . . Mr. money, money, dirty money, Cash. He's a grand old guy. . . . That's what everybody thinks."

"Shut up, Damn it. Shut up!" Second Mate grabbed George by the arm.

George jerked away from Second Mate and plopped his rear on the gunnel, facing him.

"Don't tell me to shut up, damn it. I get tired of bein'

told to shut up. Everyone tells me what to do."

Second Mate stood glaring at him.

"Don't you tell me to shut up . . . never, ever, again," George said in a slurred manner, but in a lower voice. He started to get up and plopped down again.

Second Mate shook his head in disgust and continued swabbing the deck.

Tim and Hank straining to hear all going on, remained in their perched positions.

George raised his voice again. "You got everything. Look at this boat you own. Go fishin' any time you want. . . ." He belched loudly. "I ain't got nothin'."

"Wow, he's soused," Hank whispered.

"Shusssh."

Second Mate glared menacingly at George.

"You know what? I got a great idea," George shouted. "We gotta catch us some of those great big old fishes. You know. Like one of them Flipper fishes." George stood up, turned around, and sat down again on the gunnel. "Dolphins . . . yeah, dolphins."

Tim and Hank listened intently, as before.

George continued. "Anyway, we teaches them fishes to swallow them bags we're gonna be gettin', and poop' em out when they's get back home Friday night. . . . No risk . . . Our money . . . See?" He restarted his made-up tune while laughing loudly. "Cash. He's got all the money. We does the dirty work and he gets the money."

"Holy, crap. Did ya hear that? I'll bet on eatin' a grasshopper if'n they ain't carrying dope in that thing under their boat," Tim whispered to Hank.

She agreed by nodding.

Second Mate suddenly became aware of Jasper's toolbox on the finger pier. He jumped up, lunged for George, grabbed him by the shirt pulling him up from his perch. "That box ain't yours, is it?"

George raised his head to look at it. "Nope. I . . ."

Second Mate slammed his hand over George's mouth as he then noticed the unzipped canvas tent on the large boat adjacent to them.

George's face paled and his eyes expressed fear.

Tim and Hank glared at each other.

Hank gasped. "Aw, God. We're had."

They both anxiously peeked through the window seeing Jasper approaching.

Jasper arrived, offering a greeting to the next-slip neighbors. "Afternoon. Anythin' wrong?"

Second Mate began laughing heartily. "Been fishin'. My buddy, here, had too much beer. Can you give me a hand gettin' him off the boat?"

"Sure. Yes, siree, sir. Soon's I gets these parts on the boat." Jasper boarded the boat with the parts and reached back out of the canvas tent to retrieve his tool box and sat it inside.

A look of relief appeared on Second Mate's and George's faces.

Tim and Hank laid flat on their backs on the deck of the flying-bridge trying to suppress their elation of relief. They looked at each other.

"Phewww . . . ," Tim uttered.

Jasper climbed onto the finger pier and helped get George off the Fishing Boat. Second Mate, with his hand on George's shoulder guided him down the dock, as Jasper disappeared beneath the canvas tent once again.

He hovered over his toolbox as Tim and Hank scurried down the ladder from the flying-bridge, surprising Jasper.

Hank landed on the aft deck with a thud.

"Lawd, a'mercy, child. Ya done almost scared me half to death. I done thoughts youse was gone."

"Here's your sandwich and tea. The change is in the bag. And, thanks."

Tim and Hank make a beeline for the opening in the canvas

tent.

"Wha, . . . young'un. Where's yous two travelin' to, so fast?"

Neither one of them attempted to respond.

Tim and Hank ran from the pier and across the street to the parking lot. They spot a local constable walking from the restaurant to a his police car and start hollering to get his attention.

As they approached, Hank, panting, asked Tim, "Sure ya wanna do this?"

Puffing even harder, Tim responded, "We gotta try . . ."

The Constable, a gangly hayseed of a man, hesitated from getting into his car. Tim and Hank reached him rambling on in an excited and incoherent conversation about what they've just experienced.

"Hey. Hey. Hey, . . . slow down, now. I cain't tell a word you're a'saying." The Constable pointed to Tim. "You, first."

Still excited, Tim pleaded. "Please, listen to us. We know some guys that are doin' somethin' really bad. They's workin' fer Mr. Cash. They's runnin' dope we think."

"Ain't no doubt about it. They've been usin' a super boat to bring in their stuff in the middle of the night," Hank added.

The Constable, shook his head and tried to suppress a laugh. "That's a good'un, if'n I ever heard one. . . . Cash . . . dope? You kids are way outta line."

"I knew this idiot wasn't gonna believe us. Let's get the hell outta here," Hank said.

They took off on a dead run straight for the woods on the other side of the parking lot.

"Hey. Git back here. I ain't done with you two."

Tim and Hank ran helter-skelter through the woods and reeds and, suddenly, they run smack-dab into Skull. He caught Tim in his arms.

"Oh, Gawd. I thought I'd never the day would come

when I'd ever want to see ya, agin."

Skull smiled broadly and let him go.

"Ya gotta help us. Ya gotta. Ya just gotta," Hank begged, practically out of breath.

Skull pounded his fist against his chest and then made a gesture with his hands in a palms-down motion.

Tim felt equally spent. "Ya . . . Ya want us to calm down?"

Skull nodded his head affirmatively in a decisive manner. Tim and Hank followed his lead and sat on the ground facing each other.

"I hope ya understand. . . . We been hearin' and seein' stuff nobody'll believe." Tim paused to catch his breath. "We wanted ta tell Jasper, but we jest couldn't. He'd jest be a'tellin' us we didn't know from nothin'."

"Yeah. And, we even tried to tell a cop," Hank added.

Skull waved his hand first in a stopping manner, then waved them in a manner pulling his arms to himself.

"Tim. I think he means he wants us to tell him what happened."

"I know we ain't makin' much sense, and I know you're havin' trouble understandin'. It's hard fer us, too."

Skull shook his head no, and repeated his gesture to tell him what happened.

"He wants us to tell him, not just go on gibberin'. Try tellin' somebody that Mr. Cash, the most well-known and respected man in Deale, is screwin' up. And, he's makin money off somethin' really wrong . . . maybe drugs."

Skull pointed his finger to his eyes and then to the side of his head, shaking his head in a distinctively positive manner as he arose.

"Ya know. Holy, cow. Ya know. Ya seen somethin', too," Tim said ecstatically.

Skull smiled.

"Uncle James. He's the only one that'll believe and help us. Ya have'ta take us to see him. Ya jest have'ta.

87

Somethin' awful bad's gonna happen this Friday night."

Skull nodded okay. He bent down on one knee, picked up a stick and drew a circle in the dirt with some short lines as if it represented the numbers on a clock.

Excitedly, Tim said, "That's a clock. . . . What time you talkin' about? When the crime's gonna happen?"

Skull shook his head, no. He moved his arms as if he were rowing and then did a pointing motion in the direction of the Eastern Shore.

"I think he wants to know when do we want to go see your Uncle James."

Skull shook his head yes rather vigorously, emphasized by a huge smile as Tim moved around to look at the dirt drawing from Skull's perspective.

"It says seven o'clock. You'll meet us at seven?"

Skull frowned and shook his head no, jabbing at the lower line with his stick.

"Eight o'clock?" Hank asked.

Skull looked at Hank and nodded yes with a great big smile. He pointed his finger to the sun, then moved it quickly downward to point at the ground.

"Oh, you mean tonight," Tim said.

Skull nodded yes again.

CHAPTER X

Darn the Torpedoes; Full Speed Ahead

Skull's boat arrived at the Lagoon as it was just getting dark. As they reached the shore, Tim and Hank jumped out and, in a frenzy, ran for the sailboat's aft deck.

As they scurried down the steps to the lower cabin area, Captain James sat at the galley table behind his typewriter.

Captain James looked up in a manner as if he wasn't the least bit surprised to see them.

"Hi, Uncle James."

Captain James motioned with his hand for them to take the bench seat across from him without saying a word. Hank and Tim immediately obeyed.

Skull arrived and plopped himself into Captain James' favorite overstuffed rocker-recliner.

"I thought I told you two to stay away from those bad ones," the Captain said with his eyebrows arched.

"We did, Sir. We done just want ya told us to do," Tim replied.

"Hummmmph . . ."

"We couldn't help what we overheard. . . . But, Uncle James, how'd ya know about us comin' and about the bad ones?"

"Ain't much that gets past me, son . . . really not much."

Tim related their experience, with an occasional input by Hank, as Captain James sat quietly digesting every word.

"So, ya see, Uncle James. We jest don't know what to

do. Nobody will believe us. . . . Nobody. We gotta do somethin' to stop 'em."

"Just ain't right," Hank added.

Captain James leaned back and pulled a long drag on the pipe clenched between his teeth. Then, he sat upright, taking the pipe in his hand. "'Tis a tall soundin' story, it is. And, it be a fair bet most would favor denyin' it. . . . That is, . . . all, but me.

Captain James slid from his seat, moved across to a cabinet, removed a tin of tobacco, and carried it back to the table. He sat back down and began cleaning out his pipe into an ashtray. "Ne'er did put much stock in ol' Horace Cash. . . . That be his first name, you know. . . . He be the kind to do somethin' sneakin', the ways I sees it. Aw, but you're right, all right. Church deacon . . . big-cheese Elk . . . small town Mayor, . . . he been 'em all. Ain't many would risk puttin' a finger on him." Captain James started refilling his pipe from the tin.

Tim and Hank listened intently.

Skull's head laid back and he was sound asleep; an occasional nasal snort proved him to be alive.

"Help ya, I will. What you be wantin' me to do? You have a plan?"

Tim and Hank looked at each other with big grins, then, refocused their attention on Captain James.

"Ya know we got your rail boat in the water and a'runnin'. Well, me and Hank thought this Friday night we'd . . ."

* * *

The rail boat could barely be seen sitting in the night and dark waters of the Creek -- the bow pointed at the far shore toward Tracy's Marina and Boat Yard. All was silent except for the sound of an occasional slap of water against the hull.

The cabin interior was even darker and illuminated only by lights from the far shore.

Tim and Hank sat quietly in the helm seats gazing through the opened windshield area.

The florescent dial of a windup clock sitting on the dashboard glowed the hour nearing midnight.

Hank whispered, "I thought they were gonna be here, by now."

"Me, too."

A dull thud sounded against the side of the rail boat.

"They're here."

Hank and Tim leaped from their seats and rushed to the aft deck.

Skull's boat had pulled along side, and he was tying a rope to one of the cleats as Captain James climbed aboard with Skull right behind. They immediately entered the Bridge area. With his braided cap in hand, there is just enough headroom for Captain James to stand erect. Skull is forced to bend over to remain standing.

"Here. Y'all sit down. We can use the floor."

Captain James moved to one helm seat, Skull to the other. Tim and Hank plopped on the floor, leaning their backs against the cabin wall.

Captain James's eyes scanned the boat. "From what I can tell, you've done a fine job, lad. . . . You be a Sawyer, for sure."

Tim beamed with pride. "Thanks, sir. Hank and me done
worked real hard on her."

Captain James stood and looked out of the port window, turned, and showed growing concern.

"Hummmmph . . . There's somethin not right, there is."

"Wha . . . What's wrong?" Hank asked anxiously.

"Skull. Why don't you give the anchor line a tug or two.

Skull left the bridge, and could be seen walking the gunnel to the bow through the windows. He gave a few tugs on the anchor line, stood and tried to rock the boat from side-to-side, and returned.

"How long's the boat been here?" Captain James asked, breaking the silence.

"Since late this afternoon," Tim said.

Captain James smiled. "Y'all been waitin' all that time?"

"Yes, sir. We figured it best to move her when there be other boats a'movin, too. We wouldn't draw as much attention as, we might doin it later after dark." Tim rose to his feet, stretching his arms.

"Good thinkin, but there is a problem. . . . The boat's in a bit too close to shore. The tide went out and she's sittin on the bottom."

Tim agonized. "Gawd, I'm dumb. Gawd. What we gonna do?"

Captain James reached into his pocket and pulled out his pipe, stuck it between his teeth, and lit it. Calmly he replied, "Did mud churn when you pulled up?"

"No, sir. I'm sure it didn't."

Captain James drew a long drag from the pipe. "Well, . . . the tide's been comin back in for a good while. She might break loose in a bit."

"But, we cain't ram Cash's boat if'n we cain't move her. What else can we do?"

The clock on the dash read one o'clock.

"We'll give her another fifteen minutes and then go to Plan B."

"Plan B? What's Plan B?" Hank asked.

Captain James chuckled as he drew another puff. "Well, best I can figure, we'll just have to use Skull's boat and try and block her in the boathouse channel. . . . Now, here's what we'll . . .

* * *

Cash's sleek Cabin Cruiser rested in a cradle hanging from the freighter's crane. The ship's crew were busily attaching the torpedo-like capsule to the keel. First Mate and Second Mate stood by watching.

The ship's Captain approached, speaking in a strong Latin-American accent. "How's eet progressing?"

"Okay, I guess. Look's like we're running close to schedule. No real hitches so far," First Mate responded.

"Senor, there is one now. We monitored a distress call from near Tilghman's Island. The boat drop will be delayed a half-hour, at least. We do not take chance on Coast Guard being in area."

"Nuts . . ."

The Captain smiled. "Do not be impatient. There have been many dry-runs to know it will be fine. Tonight you should be happy and celebrate. Soon, we all will be rich."

"Yeah," First Mate said half-heartedly.

The Captain walked to the cruiser and inspected the capsule
under the boat, patting it with his hand, and turned with a big
smile on his face.

* * *

Tim and Hank stood on the aft deck leaning over the gunnel holding Skull's boat lines as he and Captain James settle themselves.

Captain James took a seat at the rear of the boat as Skull sat in the center, adjusting a pair of oars.

"You'll be seein' 'em comin' long 'fore we can. Remember, now. The first thing you do is give us two flashes on the flashlight. I'll call the police and the Coast Guard on my ship-to-shore radio as soon as you do. They should have plenty of time to get here."

Tim and Hank threw the lines into Skull's boat as Captain James pushed off from the rail boat.

"Then, you young'un just sit back and watch. You hear? You don't go doin' nothin' foolish."

"Yes, sir."

Tim and Hank watched Skull's boat disappear into the night.

The clock on the dashboard read two thirty-five. Tim and Hank both stood on the port side gazing intently out of the windows, searching for the first sign of Cash's Boat.

"They should'a been here, by now," Hank whispered, showing restlessness.

Tim whispered in return. "Yeah. . . . Maybe we goofed. Wait. There . . . there they come."

Hank became excited. "I'm headin' to the bow with the light."

"I'll start the engines. Pull up the anchor line."

Hank hurried to the bow, flashing the light twice, as Tim cranked the engines. The port engine roared to life, followed by the starboard engine. The motors purred in harmony with a low rumbling sound.

* * *

Skull's boat rested against the shore in a niche slightly beyond where Hank and Tim had earlier visited. Captain James and Skull are tense and ready to move, when they hear the rail boat's engines are heard in the distance.

"Gol'dang, them young'uns. Should'a known they'd try somethin'."

* * *

Tim watched through the front window opening as she continued to pull in the anchor. "Hurry up," he called out.

"She's up."

"Hold on. I'll give her a try." Tim shoved both gear shifts forward at the same time and then slowly eased forward on the throttles.

* * *

Cash's boat moved slowly past Tracy's Creek entrance buoy, entering the last leg of its trip to the boathouse.

"Damn. I'm sure glad it's almost done," Second Mate said with a sign of relief.

"You've got that right," First Mate concurred.

* * *

The rail boat shuttered under the engines' strain. Suddenly, it began to slide slowly forward.

Hank cheered. "All right . . ." She took a shortcut across the roof of the lower cabin area and scooted through the open front windows as the rail boat broke entirely free of the chastising mud.

Tim ceased the acceleration and placed the gears in neutral. The rail boat sat idly waiting in the water. "Ya okay?"

Hank slipped off the dashboard and landed on the bridge deck. She quickly climbed into her helm seat. "Skinned my dern knee, but I'll live."

Tim maneuvered the rail boat into position, waiting for the perfect moment to make their move. The engines continuing their low rumble.

Cash's boat made its turn to approach the boat yard, when the increased roar of the rail boat's engines make it apparent it was on its way. The craft rushed out of the dark and ran head-on into the starboard side of Cash's boat driving it sideways in the water.

Second Mate fell overboard from the aft deck as First Mate bounced around inside of the smaller craft's bridge area.

Sirens and flashing police lights came from the shore as numerous squad cars quickly arrived at the Boat Yard. The police immediately swarmed over the place taking Cash's cohorts into custody.

A whooping siren and spotlights emanating from a fast approaching Coast Guard Cutter focused on Cash's boat.

* * *

Skull and Captain James detect Mr. Cash as he crawled through the hole in the fence and stumbled into Boat Yard's refuse pile of trash. As he tries to escape down the shoreline, Skull intercepts him.

Skull had him by the back of his suit coat practically off the ground by the time Captain James arrived.

"Well, what do we have here, Skull. Looks like a rat to me." He laughed. Skull grinned. "What happened to that nice new suit you be a'wearin'? Seems like you done got it all dirty."

"Go to hell. I thought you were dead."

"Maybe I am, . . . maybe I ain't. I just might be a ghost who's come back to haunt ya."

* * *

The Coast Guard cutter arrived at the scene and its crewmen pulled Second Mate from the water and boarded Cash's boat – tying lines to it. They easily apprehended First Mate.

Hank and Tim, with arms around each other's shoulders, watched from the rail boat's aft deck.

* * *

Rockhold Creek appeared unusually inactive of water traffic considering it happened to be a Saturday afternoon. Most of the shops had closed for the big celebration.

Happy Harbor's bar and restaurant was near empty as the street of the small town filled with parked cars -- everyone headed for the Elks Club. Hundreds already swarmed over the grounds with even more arriving and walking the roadways.

A huge banner reading 'Local Heroes Celebration' hung across the top of the Elks Club building. There was an abundance of food and drink tents with a bluegrass band playing.

Aunt Maggie rested in her wheelchair sitting next to Aunt Nell -- Agnes Jamison, with Captain James, standing behind.

Skull milled through the crowd with a big proud smile getting a ton of congratulations and back slaps.

* * *

Inside the Elks Club, a few old-timers remained at the bar watching a baseball game on TV. The billiards room proved empty, and the kitchen, as well.

A long center hallway lead to a banquet and dance hall where Tim sat alone on a fold-up chair at the far end of the large room.

A side door opened and Hank appeared in a brand new dress,
followed by the Elks Club manager.

Tim stood as they neared. "Ya . . . Ya sure look, uh, nice."

"Thanks. Ya look okay, too."

They remained gazing at each other.

"It's time you make your grand appearance," the manager said.

"You up to this?" Hank asked with a mischievous grin.

"Reckon we gotta."

Tim and Hank quietly followed the manager to a pair of double doors on the rear wall. As he opened them, they stepped through into the bright sunlight resulting in resounding cheers and tumultuous applause.

They looked at each other, and Tim proclaimed, "We gotta do this more often."

They gave each other a big grin, and both of them shouted, "Yes!" . . . with a pump of their fists.

THE END

ABOUT THE AUTHOR

Ever since reading Tom Sawyer as a young teenager Twain's literary mastery and cast of colorful characters has been remembered over the many years. While living in Deale, Maryland, during the late eighties and early nineties, the sedate small Chesapeake Bay community offered a setting for many tales of many genres.

Tracy's Landing is an adventurous result of both the area's conducive environment and its creative author.

www.ingramcontent.com/pod-product-compliance
Lightning Source LLC
Chambersburg PA
CBHW031854170626
46807CB00004B/1721